One Bet

Frat House Scandal

Book 1

Summer Cooper

Lovy Books

Copyright © Lovy Books Ltd, 2022. All Rights Reserved.

Summer Cooper has asserted her right under the Copyright, Designs and Patents Act 1988 to be identified as the author of this work.

This book is a work of fiction. Names and characters are the product of the author's imagination and any resemblance to actual persons, living or dead, is entirely coincidental.

In no way is it legal to reproduce, duplicate, or transmit any part of this document in either electronic means or in printed format. Recording of this publication is strictly prohibited and any storage of this document is not allowed unless with written permission from the publisher. All rights reserved.

Respective authors own all copyrights not held by the publisher.

Lovy Books Ltd
20-22 Wenlock Road
London N1 7GU

Cover by SC Creative

Chapter 1

Avery

Maybe it was the fall air, it always smelled of pumpkin spice and campus bonfires. Or perhaps it was the homecoming week celebrations, I wasn't sure, but something about this time of year, even a decade ago when I was the one attending Glouster University, sucked. Now that I was Professor Avery Stroh at the same university, I had to pretend to enjoy the festivities. I had to act as if I was proud of the returning alumni. This year sucked even more than previous homecoming festivities though, because all I could think about was how I would rather not celebrate the one-hundredth anniversary of the Alpha Alpha Phi fraternity, at all. I would rather forget it altogether.

I sat in the commons of the admissions building, a century-old brick monster with high ceilings and carved wood banisters, handing out goody bags with the usual college swag, a t-shirt, key chain, and personal alarm all with the Glouster crest emblazoned on their surfaces, to students past and present, with a fake smile that said I didn't have a care in the world. That smile hid the hurricane inside of me, that college senior, torn apart, lied to, hellbent on taking the Alphas down. And I'd tried. I still had a copy of my infamous revenge article framed at home.

Back then, I'd been the girl voted most likely to cut someone, not that I would have. But girls who wore thick lines of black eyeliner

One Bet

to match their fishnet stockings, combat boots, and corset tops, with more tattoos and piercings than appendages to put them on, always tended to get the bad rap, and that was me. Although my clothes, back then, weren't an expression of who I was, just an expression of what I could afford and make work.

Now I dressed like a teacher: jeans and sweaters, scarves and boots. I stopped dying my long brown hair, and either tied it back or left it straight, and I worked out Tuesday and Friday mornings. I wasn't scary. I wasn't beautiful. I was boring, and it worked for me. Until now.

"Hi, Avery."

Oh God, his voice hadn't changed. I looked up slowly, taking in every inch of him I could see above the table I sat behind. Because of his height, somewhere in the 6'4" – 6'5" range, I could see plenty, and it was still divine. Long legs, tapered waist, with rock-hard abs I could see under his tight white shirt. Honey-colored hair and denim blue eyes. Oh God, again. He was still amazing, and my 22-year-old heart banged like a drum inside my 32-year-old chest.

"Keaton." I tried to say it with a smile, but I probably looked as constipated as my clenched stomach made me feel. I thrust a bag toward him, and he grabbed it before I managed to punch it into his gut. "Here you go. Enjoy your homecoming."

To my credit, I didn't sound like I'd eaten gravel or that I'd spent the last decade working as a phone sex operator, which I hadn't, but sometimes sounded as if I had. And either one was as likely as the other since he still reminded me of all those feelings he'd inspired before. Lust, attraction, love.

My practiced greeting should've been it, should've been enough. It was for me anyway. I didn't need him to cover my hand with his for me to remember his touch. I didn't need him to smile for me to recall the beauty of it and I damned sure didn't need to breathe in the scent of his cologne for me to want to close my eyes and inhale him. But in that one shaky second, all those things happened.

I jerked away because preserving my sanity and not making a scene in front of the people who controlled everything from my salary to my living quarters made more sense than whatever stupid thing my body and heart would have led me to do if I kept touching him.

He curled his fingers around the bag and smiled at me. Ten years ago, I would've swooned. Today, I was stronger and smarter. There would be no swooning, not until I was in the privacy of my own cottage resentfully reliving every millisecond of this meeting, at least.

"You look good." And he smiled, the bastard.

But I had no desire to reciprocate the thought or tell him something the world already knew. "Thanks, so do you."

That was what he did to me. He removed all the conscious thought and reasonably intelligent intentions from my brain with one smile.

"Maybe we could get together this week? Catch up on old times."

Our old times consisted of two glorious weeks that I hadn't realized were glorious back then, a night on his dad's yacht, and my broken heart. No way was I getting together to catch up on anything. "Sure."

I wanted to tape my own mouth shut. "Good. I'll find you." He always managed that particular feat back then and I had no doubt he would know exactly where I would be when he wanted to see me.

He flashed another smile, the heartbreaker that made my knees jelly and my heart a jackhammer, then turned and walked toward the door. Shamefully, I watched every move. This was a man who didn't just walk, he glided like he had a cloud under his feet propelling him forward. It was either a trick of lighting or a figment of my imagination. I never, even now, knew which.

I spent the rest of the afternoon handing out bags and penciling in names before my shift at the table was over. Not that I remembered much of it. I'd been too busy trying and failing not to think of Keaton for that to work.

There was so much to remember, so many things about him that I might've forgotten if not for my broken heart. I had managed to shove them to the far recesses of my mind, but since this afternoon, I couldn't seem to think of anything else and it all came back with shocking clarity.

One Decade Ago

I was an addict, not in the traditional do drugs, love alcohol kind of way. But in the must stare, must drool over Ryder Kennedy kind of way.

Ryder wasn't just extraordinary and amazing; he was the epitome of whatever level existed above extraordinary and amazing. He had the hair, the eyes, the swagger of a man who already knew his place in the world and was out to claim it and anything that stood in his way. Didn't hurt that he was a football star and leader of the Alpha Alpha Phi fraternity. He also had a reputation for dating Sigmas, the most elite sorority on campus, a sorority that took one look at me freshman year and passed. Hard.

It made more than one girl try her hand at rushing the Sigmas. I was no exception; I didn't give two shits about being a Sigma except for the fact that eventually, Ryder would work his way around to dating me. Pathetic, and I knew it, but that didn't stop me from doing my damnedest to fit in with them. But I was the girl at the school only because she'd gotten a hardship scholarship to pad out her financial aid. The girl that bought her cardigans at the thrift store, and who didn't know how to hold her pinky out when she sipped her tea from their fine china cups. I didn't have a chance. I gave up and went back to my combat boots and torn fishnets, content to ogle Ryder from afar and hate the Sigmas from my pedestal on the school newspaper.

Today, I was in my Film Studies class, more than happy to ignore *My Fair Lady* on the projection screen and doodle *Mrs. Ryder Kennedy* and *Mrs. Avery Stroh Kennedy* with the requisite hearts and flowers on the corner of the handout sheet that detailed the project due next week.

"Hey, Avery, you have a pen?"

Ugh. Keaton Shaw. Another Alpha. Almost as pretty as Ryder, but not so…Ryder. He wasn't blonde but had honey-colored locks a little too long and designed to look unkempt. His eyes weren't green, but a light blue that didn't glow or dance or sparkle. Okay. I could admit he had a nice body. But he wasn't Ryder. Even though he did talk to me on occasion.

I handed him a Bic from my purse then went back to my doodles.

"Mr. Shaw?" Our teacher, at the front of the class, smiled in our direction. "Agree or disagree?"

Fuck, I was glad he'd called on Keaton and not me. I hadn't heard the question. "I'm sorry. I was getting a pen."

"Henry Higgins. Narcissist or not?"

I watched Keaton struggle. I'd seen this movie a hundred times. It was an old favorite. I nodded slightly, trying for covert, but Professor Weller caught me. "Miss Stroh believes he is. Help him out, Miss Stroh."

"Classic narcissist. His way was the only way even though she asked for his help. Higgins built himself into an important person, so he didn't have to be vulnerable with his personal self. He changed Eliza into something acceptable to him, what he wanted her to be, rather than letting her find and be happy with herself." I spoke as if I was bored, but I thoroughly believed in what I was saying. "In the end, she got her guy but at what cost to herself thanks to him."

Sadly, the part of the statement that stuck out for me was that she'd gotten her man. And that, again sadly, was where the worst idea of my life came from.

Chapter 2

Keaton

I knew she'd be here, knew she'd look beautiful and I also knew she would smell like flowers and sunshine. But it still knocked the wind out of me. It still reminded me of the one night we spent together, when I held her, and we talked about a thousand unimportant things and the one thing I'd felt for her all along. Best night of my life, bar none.

But right now, I had a splitting headache, a less than suitable perk of being a quarterback for the Alabama Knights with an offensive line that allowed more sacks than any other in the NFL. Or maybe the memory of seeing her face when I walked in was more responsible than the recent concussion that had me sidelined.

Today, I didn't have time for a headache, or time to find a dark room and sleep it off. I had parties to attend, glory days to celebrate with Finn, Jameson, maybe even Ryder, although I wanted to see him less than the others, way less. Okay, not at all. I walked toward the Alpha house, if any of the guys were there, we could get a drink, that would help.

Not much had changed about the house. It was still brick, although thanks to Ryder, the front had been painted more than once. Bushes lined the property on each side and there were still guys throwing around a football on the front lawn, a keg on the porch, and music coming from the back patio. There'd been a lot of good times in this house, a lot of parties and a lot of girls.

I turned up the walk and one of the guys on the lawn called my name and threw the ball at me. I lifted my hands in just enough time to catch it. Once upon a time, I'd been great, recognized everywhere. But thanks to injuries, new and more talented guys, and a roster full of second-stringers ready to make their mark, I spent a lot of time wearing a headset on the sidelines. It had been a while since I'd touched pigskin anywhere except practice, but today it didn't matter. Here, I was a hero. A guy who'd made it and it felt good. I threw the ball back and smiled at the cheer from the watchers, it was like I'd thrown the game-winning Super Bowl touchdown.

Before I made it to the door, I was surrounded by a new breed of Alpha Alpha Phi brothers, all younger, all athletes. By comparison, I was exactly what the Sunday commentators said, a used-up has been, past his prime and ready for retirement. Fuck, maybe being back wasn't the great idea I'd thought it would be. It certainly wasn't helping my morale.

But I would eat up their adoration until they figured out, I was on my way out of the pros. I signed a few autographs, then walked up to the porch where Finn waited. "About time." He shook my hand and slapped my shoulder.

"I got sidetracked." I nodded to the yard where beers were being passed around. A normal Friday afternoon at Alpha house.

Finn laughed. "Yeah. I saw your distraction at the registration table. She's looking good." A tinge of jealousy spread through my gut. Finn didn't need to be looking at Avery. No one did. "She single?"

Fuck, what if she wasn't? What if she was married with kids and a life? What if she hadn't spent the last ten years pining over me, comparing every man to me and finding him lacking, the way I had been pining for her and shading women when they failed to measure up to the woman I'd never stopped thinking about? For all I knew, she could've been married with ten kids, one for each year we'd been apart, the doting husband, and some adorable dog that only loved her.

"I don't know."

"Did you talk to her?" He handed me a bottle of a craft brew then kicked back in one of the chairs beside the keg and various coolers.

I shrugged. My lame attempt at chit-chat hardly counted as talking to her, but Finn didn't have to know how badly I'd fumbled. "Not really."

"You think she still has that bike?"

The Harley, we'd taken a few rides on it back when she didn't hate me, back when she'd been free-spirited and happy. Before Ryder destroyed all of that and she tried to destroy us in return. Before I could answer, a couple of other guys from our days at Glouster walked out of the house. There were more man hugs and welcome backs, but my heart wasn't in it, I was busy remembering the girl with the motorcycle and combat boots.

One Decade Ago

The proposition was intriguing. And it would save my ass. But Avery Stroh didn't know, didn't understand all that she would have to do, or what she would go through if Ryder got a hold of her. None of them did. They all saw him as some kind of god, but in truth, he was just an asshole. He had always been one of those silver spoon boys with no moral compass and no sense of the damage he left in his wake.

Finn and I sat in lawn chairs on one side of the cooler while Jameson and Ryder sat on the other and five or six pledges in diapers painted the front of the house. Fourth time this month we'd had to cover the word *Asshole* someone had painted onto the brick. *Someone* being one of Ryder's scorned women, not that we ever knew which one. There were too many suspects and not enough interest in finding which one it was since the hardware store was never going to run out of coverup and we were never going to run out of pledges to do the job.

Finn chuckled. "You could've gotten them bigger paintbrushes." Right now, they'd covered the A, the H, and part of the E because Ryder had supplied them with half-inch brushes. This was going to take forever, someone was going to have to make a beer run if they didn't hurry up.

I would have laughed along because it was expected, but I was too busy thinking about Avery, more fantasizing about her, about smelling her perfume on my pillow, seeing her black hair fanned out beneath her as I lowered my head and…

Finn nudged my shoulder as a sleek black motorcycle rolled up at the edge of the lawn. "Who is that?"

I knew her right away, torn black jeans,

battered black leather jacket, boots that laced up from ankle to calf with a square heel and a steel toe. Normally, I preferred the typical co-ed with the ponytails and Lululemon leggings. But something about Avery Stroh made my dick harder than it had been in a while. And she hadn't even touched me yet.

Avery shut off the bike and removed her helmet, shaking her hair out while simultaneously using her foot to put down the kickstand. It was a lot of bike for a woman so small, but she handled it like she'd been born on it. I stood and walked toward her. When she'd asked for my assistance in exchange for homework help, she'd been honest. More honest than anyone I'd ever met, especially considering the subject matter and her ultimate goal.

She nodded to the house. "You guys paint a lot."

"Yeah." She had the smoothest voice of anyone I knew. I cleared my throat and stared.

Up close, she was more than beautiful. Clear gray eyes, not boring gray, more like storm clouds rolling in, and her hair was board straight and hung to the middle of her back in a color so deep and dark it looked like satin. I shook my head, this was no time to be lusting after a woman who wanted one of my very best friends. "So, I thought about your…idea. Are you sure this is what you want?"

She looked over my shoulder, and I didn't have to guess at who. She bit her lip and smiled. "Yeah. I'm sure."

I knew I should say no, I knew this was the worst idea in the history of ideas. "Okay."

And so, it started, the beginning of the most beautiful and the most devastating relationship of my life.

Chapter 3

Avery

Home sweet home, no more classes, or students, no more meetings with the department head. Just me, a glass of wine, and a bubble bath in my little faculty cottage. Three rooms and a bathroom with a clawfoot tub, enough for me.

I twisted the nozzle marked hot then added some Tahitian Dream bubbles into the pooling water and stripped out of my skirt and sweater, just as the doorbell rang.

Shit. Shit. Shit. I ran down a list of suspects, Mom was in Atlanta and she wouldn't dare, nor could she afford to spring a surprise trip north. Dad was…well, I didn't know but Maine was as unlikely as anywhere else in the world since he'd left twenty-five years ago and hadn't been back since. My one friend, Alex Rhodes, wasn't due in town until tomorrow. That left either a prank knock or the religious spreaders of the 'Good News'. But damn, I had to answer.

I pulled a towel around me, tucked the tab in over my heart, and walked across the living room to the door. Before I opened it, I checked the peephole, and my heart stumbled, it might have even fallen into my stomach.

Keaton Shaw, what the hell was he doing at my door?

"I'm busy." And wearing a towel and definitely not in the mood for a walk down any memory lane that involved him. As such, an act of God wouldn't be enough to convince me to open the damned door.

"Avery." The way he said my name, soft and low, still gave me goosebumps, still made me want to purr.

Okay, so an act of God wouldn't do it, but his voice did. I yanked the door open a few inches, enough to poke my head out without giving him a view of my towel. "Why are you here?" Blunt, harsh, and to the point. Maybe there was some of the old me left, after all.

He chuckled. "There she is, the girl I met in Film Studies class. That's the girl I haven't stopped thinking about in ten years." He pulled a pen out of his back pocket, a blue Bic he could've bought anywhere, but a little part of me hoped he hadn't just stopped at the campus store on the way over. "You know what this is?"

He leaned his head against the doorframe, and because of my unwillingness to open the door, we were nose to nose. I could see every fleck of dark blue in his light blue eyes. "It's your pen. I kept it all these years."

Though, by the smell of him, this conversation was inspired by a few too many Bud Lights, his smile melted my...well, everything. "Keaton, go home. You're drunk."

"My home is lonely." He sighed and moved back and leaned his head against the doorframe. "Are you married, Avery?"

"No." There was no point in asking him if he was. If the great Keaton Shaw dared tie the knot, a hundred different tabloids would have been on hand to report on the bride's designer dress, the exotic locale, the way the sun made the day brighter and the groom couldn't keep his eyes or his hands off the bride. They certainly played show and tell with the harem of women he dated.

"But I have a boyfriend." No, I didn't. Not even a prospect.

"Oh." He pushed to stand almost straight, stumbled, and I flung the door open to step out and hold him up. He wrapped both arms around my waist and pulled me into his chest, suddenly quite able to stand strong and sturdy.

"You have a boyfriend?" He puffed out his lower lip as if pouting. "Damn it."

I pulled away, now holding onto my towel. We were standing on my front porch on a street populated by faculty, the last thing I needed was to be seen groping the alumni hero. "You should go."

He looked around me to the inside of my cottage. "Is he here? Can I meet him?"

Shit. Shit. Shit. "Um, no. He isn't here, he'll be in town tomorrow." Alex would go along with my ruse if I asked him and I would because no way could I be the pathetic one. Plus, it was only for a week, at least, I hoped so.

"We should get drinks. I'd love to meet him." He had a twinkle in his eye and my stomach leaped. Some things never changed and apparently, my reaction to his pretty face was one of those things.

"I think you've had enough to drink."

He reached to tuck a piece of hair behind my ear and I shivered at the unexpected familiarity of his touch. "I remember when it was you who had too much to drink and I took care of you."

Yeah. I remembered that, too. Vaguely.

One Decade Ago

The bar wasn't crowded, but it smelled like old beer, a mixture of perfume and body odor, blended in with the stench of smoke. I sat at the scarred wood counter and sipped a beer. Not because I liked it, but because to sit at the bar, I'd had to order something, and draft beer was about all I could afford.

Keaton was late, but of course he was. Sundays were for watching football with the guys. At least they were at Alpha house where every TV was tuned to the big game and testosterone demanded no one missed a single first down.

So, I waited.

I looked around the bar, this was definitely a college bar. Small dance floor, a lot of TVs, the smell of fried buffalo wings and cheesy nachos. Plus, drink specials for off days, dollar beers on Monday, two-dollar rails on Tuesdays with dollar tacos, wet T-shirt Wednesdays, Trivia Thursdays, and Touchdown Shots, or whatever they were on Sundays. Although the clientele today was more of the old folk variety.

The game was on above the bar, and I watched out of nothing more than curiosity, certainly not because I understood the allure of the game or the rules that went with it. It looked like a bunch of guys chasing each other around trying to capture a half-deflated ball, although, I did like the pants. A lot.

The few patrons at the bar erupted into cheers and the bartender, who was about my age and a tall lanky specimen of a man, filled eleven shot glasses with tequila then distributed them to each of us at the bar. He handed me a slice of lime and a saltshaker.

"I didn't order this." Nor could I pay for it, all my savings were going toward the My Fair Lady project that would turn me into Ryder's woman. Clothes. Shoes. New hair. And some makeup.

He chuckled. "Oh, darlin'. Touchdown shots are a Sunday bonus." He grinned. "Enjoy."

He held up his own glass and waited for me to clink mine against the rim.

I chuckled. "Well, in that case…"

Who was I to disappoint?

I was three touchdowns in when Keaton finally slid onto the stool next to mine. "Hey. Sorry, I'm late."

I swayed in my seat and nudged his shoulder with mine. "No problem. Alex, the bartender, and now my new best friend was just explaining the rules of football to me." Alex turned a charming shade of red and nodded at me, then glared at Keaton. I widened my eyes. "Very complicated game and not the kind of thing I usually enjoy. The tequila probably helps." I motioned to my tower of upside-down shot glasses.

Keaton chuckled, the sound rich and lush and full. "Hey, Alex the bartender. Could I get a Jack and Coke?"

Without the smile he'd been blessing me with through the last three quarters, Alex poured Keaton's drink and set it on the bar. "Six-fifty."

Keaton handed him an American Express. "Run a tab."

Then he dismissed Alex as though he was nothing more than the help and turned to me.

By the mid-fourth quarter, I was all over Keaton. Licking salt from his neck, letting my hands roam freely over his chest and back when I forced him onto the dance floor because some guy had played the jukebox. Then I let him pour me into a cab to see me home only moments after I threw up on his shoes.

And that was the reason I didn't drink anymore, not even Touchdown Shots at Alex's parents' bar.

Chapter 4

Keaton

I woke in an unfamiliar bed in an unfamiliar room, but the smell of flowers and sunshine coated the pillow and I knew exactly where I was. Usually, when this happened, there was a woman at my side, and I wore substantially less clothing, but now, I was dressed in yesterday's t-shirt and jeans with my shoes lined up at the edge of the bed.

My head ached, could've been a hangover,

or could've been my usual issue, but I sat up anyway. The alarm clock on the table read four, which could have only been a.m. considering the lack of light from outside, and I had a powerful need to bury my head in her pillow and inhale. Instead, I stood and slipped my feet into my shoes.

While I had no memory of how I ended up here or in her bed, I remembered her towel, bright orange and pulled tight around her. Most guys were into boobs and ass, but I had a thing for shoulders, the curve where they met the throat, the sleek lines leading down to the arms that had reached out to steady me, the very 3-D tattoo of a butterfly just below her collarbone. Maybe I only like Avery's shoulders, but it had been so long since another woman made me feel the way she did, I couldn't say for sure.

I also had a vague memory of standing in inches of water in her living room. Laughing together as we sopped and mopped the floor.

Oh, dear. I remembered her laugh, the melody of it. Something about Avery Stroh made me think of her with a rose-colored romantic tint. Even back when she'd been looking at me with anything but romantic intentions.

I walked out into the living room, content to sneak past her quietly and slip out before she had the chance to wake up and I might have made it had she not looked so adorable curled around a pillow on the sofa, a slight smile on her face and eyelids that fluttered as if she was dreaming. I stared for a second, decided I was being creepy, then turned back to the door. My hand touched the metal knob but didn't twist before she spoke. "Leaving so soon?"

Oh, God. I'd never done the walk of shame, particularly after nothing shameful happened. I cleared my throat. "Yeah. I figured you might want your bed back."

She sat up, adjusting a blue t-shirt that fell off one shoulder as she used her free hand to throw a blanket to the end of the couch. "Coffee for the road?"

There was no need to prolong the agony.

"I should go." But I probably needed to apologize for whatever I'd done to flood her house and…God only knew what else. "Avery, about last night…"

She cocked an eyebrow and I reconsidered my apology in favor of something that involved our lips touching and our tongues dueling and if she'd given me one other signal to go ahead, I would have marched over and laid a kiss on her that would've rocked both our worlds, but she didn't even smile. Apology, it was.

"I'm sorry for…" I wasn't even sure how much I needed to be sorry for. "Flooding your place?"

"That was me. I forgot to turn off the tub before I answered the door." She wobbled her head back and forth. "And a little bit you because you weren't the 'Good News' guys."

I didn't understand that, but it came with a

smile, so I didn't mind not knowing what she meant.

"Well, sorry anyway. And for showing up here. Uninvited." And while I was being honest… "But I didn't think an invitation would come, and I wanted to see you, but now that I know you have a boyfriend, I'll leave you alone. I don't want to ruin anything for you. Or for him."

Or for me. I wanted to get the hell off this campus and go home.

Her face went pale and her smile lost its dazzle. "I, uh, I appreciate that."

I wanted to ask her if everything was okay, more specifically if she was okay, but I didn't. I chickened out because I didn't want to hear that I was making her uncomfortable, not because I'd so much as touched her, but because I didn't belong here. "Okay. Well. I'm gonna go."

Ten years ago, I wouldn't have cared that she had a man in her life. I wouldn't have walked away either. I would have pulled her against me so our bodies lined up in all the best ways, kissed her the way I wanted to, and let her know without ever saying a word that I was here to stay, that I wanted more. I wanted the way we were the one night we spent together and maybe some of the better times of those two weeks.

One Decade Ago

Having Avery look at me with such trust was a responsibility that made my shoulders sag. How could I let her down? But damned if I wanted her to end up with Ryder. He would hurt her, it was his signature move. And it would be my fault.

But she'd dragged me to the beauty salon for her big makeover. First, they'd given her some makeup to cover up her tattoos because no

Sigma would ever desecrate her body with ink, and Ryder only dated Sigmas. But I was man enough to admit that seeing all those luscious lines and body art on Avery made my dick hard. But since she'd licked that salt off my neck at Hilly's, everything about her made my cock stand in hope of a more intimate inspection of her tats.

She looked up at me, smiled, and I almost lost my shit. I wanted to kiss her. Instead, I shoved my hands in my pockets as she held her hair out. "Blonde right? All the Sigmas are blonde?"

I shook my head. "Lacey is a brunette. Kinney is a redhead. You don't have to be a blonde, maybe you can just tone this down a little bit."

She chuckled. "I don't want to use a chunk of my savings on toning it down. I want to be bold and shocking. I want to be platinum." She would look great bald or gray-haired or however she decided. The beauty in her was more than attractive facial features, somehow though, she didn't see it.

The beautician's eyes went wide. "Are you sure, honey? It's going to take a while."

Avery nodded. "I'm positive."

It took three hours, then four, then five. The foil came off of her hair bringing the ends with it. "Shit." I couldn't help it. There were orange strands of hair sticking up, other pieces a lighter coral color trapped in the foil. I didn't know Avery's temper, from the looks of her, it would be lethal, but she just breathed out of wide-open lips.

"Oh my God. I look like a pumpkin head." Tears pooled in her eyes. "What the fuck?"

If I had to describe her tone and her eyes and the downturn of her mouth, I would have gone with hopeless.

I put a hand on her shoulder. "It's going to be okay." Not that I knew how. Hair took a while to come back and she had clumps missing and what was still there was orange and gummy looking.

She sat up.

"Easy for you to say. You're gorgeous and you get every girl you want." Her hands shook in front of her. "He's never going to look at me now. Unless it's to laugh at me."

I wanted to tell her that he was absolutely the kind of guy who would laugh at her, but I was afraid she'd call off our deal and shameful behavior or not, I still needed her help to bring up my grades so I could stay eligible to play. I looked at the stylist then back at Avery.

Probably sensing a full-on tantrum, the beautician left the shampoo room and came back not more than a second later with another woman. This one was a few years older but she had short blonde hair streaked with strands of auburn and black curled around her face. Her makeup was thick but highlighted her cheekbones, round eyes, and full lips.

"Hello. I'm Reba. Let me take a look." She

circled Avery with her index finger against her chin. "I can work with this."

Reba nodded once then ran her fingers through what was left of Avery's hair. Nothing more came off in her fingers and I breathed a silent sigh of relief. The last thing Avery needed was to see more of her hair come out, but before I could offer any reassurances, Reba spoke again.

"You have a beautiful face and you've been hiding it. I said that to Micha when you walked in, didn't I?" If she had, Micha was too stunned to do more than a nod. "I think a nice pixie cut, something like Michelle Williams favors. And don't you worry about the color. I can fix that, too. You will be rocking platinum in half an hour."

I didn't buy it, but more, Avery didn't buy it. Unless tears streaming down her cheeks and a runny nose meant she was believing in the power of this woman to work some sort of miracle, I knelt in front of her. "What do you want to do?"

"I want my hair back."

I glared at the beautician then smiled at Avery. "You know, I'm kind of glad this happened, now I can see your face, every adorable freckle, the intensity of your eyes." And because I could, I brushed my thumb over her lips. "This perfect mouth. You're beautiful, Avery, and I think you should show it off."

Even though I'd started it as nothing more than a means to make her feel better, I meant it. Now that I could see her face, I couldn't stop seeing her face. I didn't want to stop.

"Do you think Ryder will like it?"

Ryder, right, that lucky bastard. What was I thinking anyway? My lust skidded to a halt, just because I was between chicks didn't mean… anything. I pulled back and stood, crossing my arms, fighting for my reassuring smile now. "Um, yeah. Yeah. He's gonna…he's gonna love it."

She sniffed again but looked over her shoulder at Reba. "Okay. Go ahead."

Reba gently pushed Avery back so that her neck rested on the curve of the shampoo bowl, and she set to work.

An hour later, she twisted the chair so I could see Avery, and while I already knew how beautiful she was, I added a new word to my list for Avery, exquisite.

Chapter 5

Avery

I'd never been to a football game before. Not when I was in college and certainly not since, but this was the homecoming again. The "beat the Trojans" game that put all the former students in one section of the stadium and had the whole place chanting for the Glouster Gators.

The air smelled like fresh popcorn, hotdogs, and cold air. The cheers started right about the time they introduced the team that had won the last championship at Glouster; Keaton's team. From where I sat, close enough to God I could hear the angel's harps, I couldn't make out more than his shape, thank God, but my stomach still clutched when he waved to the crowd and the crowd...they were hopeful, wildly hopeful if the noise level was any indication, that this year's team would bring home another crown...or trophy...or pennant to hang.

    I didn't care, I never cared. Right now, I needed to talk to Alex, who had yet to arrive. He was twenty-seven minutes late. He probably hadn't stopped tailgating yet. And probably wouldn't until right around the fourth quarter.

    I twisted my head from one side to the other, checking both walkways that led to our seats. It wasn't until the marching band turned up for their spirited rendition of the Glouster fight song that I saw him trying to weave his way through the crowd to the seats I'd bought him and his "friend."

He leaned over and kissed my cheek, beer scenting his breath. "Hello, beautiful."

I smiled, if he could keep that kind of talk up for a couple of days, this week might not actually kill me. I had hope.

"Hey. It is so good to see you." And I meant that. After that night in his bar when we'd first met, he'd become a friend. More than that, he'd become someone I could count on even though we hardly ever managed to get together. Although we talked at least once a month, we hadn't seen each other in at least a year, I missed his smile. It was pearly white and wide. Genuine in ways people just didn't smile anymore. His smile was home to me. "So, where's your friend?"

"She made a pit stop at the bathroom."

"She?" Oh no. My plan spiraled. Circled its way from brilliant around to flop.

His skin turned the same shade of red as his shirt. "Yeah. You're gonna love her. She's a teacher, like you. She's beautiful and smart.

Actually, you might know her, she went to school here." He reached into his pocket and pulled out a black velvet box that could have only held the death to each of my hopes for the remainder of homecoming week, but I was happy for him. More happy for her when he opened the box and the sunlight hit a three-carat, at least, circle cut diamond.

"Woah. That's gorgeous." I leaned in to inspect the ring just as he snapped it closed and pulled away to shove it into his pocket. "She'd be a fool to say no."

"You think so?" I'd known Alex for years and had never seen him nervous. Ever. This guy had confidence in spades, but not the cocky kind that turned people off. He had a sexy kind of confidence made of humor, happiness, and optimism. Ordinarily, back then, and probably now if I was honest, I would have hated him for it, but no one hated Alex Rhodes. Ever.

Then I saw her, the woman of his dreams, Susie Chastain. Coming toward him and smiling as she gave him a little wave and threaded her way to the seat. She planted a kiss on him that was more appropriate for a movie love scene than a football game then she held out her hand to me. "Avery?"

"Hello, Susie." And why were we pretending we hardly knew each other? We'd been close once, bonded over our heartache.

Her eyes narrowed. "I can't believe it's you."

She slapped Alex's shoulder, and he winced. "You didn't tell me your best friend was Avery."

He widened his eyes at her, and she grinned.

If ever two people in this world belonged together it was them and I wanted to hear their story, I really did, but my head was spinning. I didn't want to be the girl who went without her fake boyfriend for the week while Keaton, still the big man on campus, flashed his pretty smile at every girl he saw while I had to watch. The pretense was better than loneliness.

Around me, the crowd stood as our receiver crossed the goal line and the referee's arms went up. The fight song blared from the band section and the ring of lights around the stadium flashed red and white. Alex grabbed Susie by the waist and kissed her, again, like they were alone and not in a crowd of at least fifty-thousand people.

But when I looked at them, not staring, just a quick glance, Susie's eyes were open and bored. Then she shot me a wink, and I knew there would be no happy engagement announcement this week. In a crowd full of people whooping and cheering, I couldn't figure out her game, but my money was on her old grudge with the Alpha fraternity that broke her heart.

One Decade Ago

One Bet

Susie tossed me a bottle of spray paint, she had neon-glow orange, and mine was flamingo pink, I could feel her anger vibrating around us as loudly as the little metal balls in our cans of paint. By morning, so long as we didn't end up in jail, the Alphas would know exactly what Susie thought about them. Although, I wouldn't have minded knowing why I was risking my scholarship, bail money I didn't have, a date I desperately wanted to get and wouldn't if I was caught, not to mention a coating of bright pink blowback for a bunch of guys who wouldn't give a shit anyway if we painted the story of the frat's whole sordid past on their house.

Susie hunched behind the bushes and peeked out like she'd taken 007 classes this semester instead of Art Appreciation. She held out her arm to keep me from moving around her where we could be seen. "There's still a light on."

It was almost four a.m., and I had an eight o'clock class. I swatted away hair I didn't have anymore and tried to straighten my cramping legs. "Why are we doing this again?"

She looked at me over her shoulder, and even in the dark of night, I could see the fury in her big brown eyes. Her voice sharpened. "Those fucking Alphas are going to pay."

Not that I didn't think they weren't mostly a bunch of self-important assholes, but clarification never hurt either. "What happened?"

"I went out with…one of them." Names, I wanted names, mostly out of curiosity. "And the son of a bitch video recorded the whole thing. As I was leaving, walking out of the Alpha house, they had it playing on the TVs in their house and they were all laughing like I was some kind of joke."

I wanted to be a good friend, sympathetic, at least, but my mind was spinning with images of Ryder. What if it was him? Or Keaton?

"What did you do?" It wasn't like I couldn't infer the details, but anything that made a girl who once upon a time only believed in peace and love go full-on graffiti-hate had to be a good story.

"I couldn't do anything but leave. I was just…devastated. I mean, we went on three dates, not really dates, more like meet-ups." She emphasized the word as if it was its own language. "But they were classy, you know? I didn't feel like he was just trying to get into my pants. It was always imported beer and gourmet picnics, never out in public, though, always on that damned boat. So, the night of the third date, we're back on the boat, of course, and it's beautiful. A crystal chandelier, flowers, and chilled champagne. We kissed in the moonlight, made love on the deck, then he asked me to spend the night with him, but he had practice in the morning so could we go back to the frat house. Of course, I said yeah." She gave me a wide-eyed can-you-believe-this-shit look. And frankly, I didn't know what to think. "So, he took me to the frat house through this private entrance."

She paused and breathed in deep so her nostrils flared and her jaw hardened. "When it was over, he got up and went for food, another one of those other bastards came in, told me not to worry, he didn't do sloppy seconds. Instead, he opened the drawer next to the bed, grabbed a twenty, and tossed it to me. Told me it was cab fare." She shook her head, her mouth thinned as she glared at me. "I couldn't get out the door we came in. I had to do the walk of shame through the house while all his friends laughed. The worst part, well aside from the way he used me and threw me out part of the night, was all my moans were at top volume. Then for a week, I had to see the hickeys he marked me with."

Oh, God. My stomach ached for her pain, for the embarrassment, for what they'd put her through, I couldn't even imagine.

But Susie wasn't done with her tale. "When

One Bet

I called him later, he didn't even take my call but had one of the other guys call me back to spew his threats. Said if I didn't shut up and go away, he'd make sure I went viral." She shook her can of paint and the ball-bearing inside rattled against the can. "I'll show these fuckers a scene."

"Susie...maybe we should..." Should what? Without the video, we couldn't prove anything and I didn't see them letting us in to do our own search for the incriminating evidence. Besides, these guys practically walked on water at Glouster. And I didn't have a rich daddy paying for my education so that I could switch schools if I got kicked out of this one for spraying graffiti on the front of a university-owned building. "Maybe call someone instead of painting the house."

A guidance counselor? The dean?

She took it as a fear for her, rather than my selfish wish to stay in school.

"I'm not afraid of him." She cocked an

eyebrow and pursed her lips. "Just because he has a big dick doesn't mean he knows what to do with it, know what I mean?"

She turned back to watch the house.

And for clarity, no, I didn't know what she meant. I hadn't done more than a little making out. Girls who looked like me didn't get a lot of dates that ended with more than a wave and a fake promise to call. But, with Keaton's help, that would all change and I was going to end up with Ryder.

Chapter 6

Keaton

Some things never change; Hilly's was one of those things. Same polished wood bar, scarred wood floors, stained wood walls, a tinder box of memories.

I taught Avery to dance here, or maybe she taught me. Her way had been more fun, anyway, if I closed my eyes, sometimes I could still feel her against me. Still smell her shampoo, still hear her soft breaths. Even after all these years.

I motioned to the bartender for another beer and tried not to think of Avery. But the creak of the arched door, old wood, older hinges, announced new arrivals, and I caught her reflection in the mirror behind the bar.

The adult version of her, long light brown hair, a conservative dress that hid the delectable tattoos I'd, once upon a time, traced with my finger then my tongue, downplayed sexuality that even her buttoned collars couldn't hide. It still affected me like I hadn't quite escaped puberty, I wanted her. Probably would never stop wanting her.

And damned if I could sit at the bar with my back to her when she was so close. I spun on my barstool, frosty mug in one hand, back against the brass rail that lined the counter. Oh, yeah. I was still *the* Keaton Shaw, laidback, friendly, confident.

Right up to the second she glanced up and our eyes met, and a thrill of electricity short-circuited my brain. I tried to wave with the hand holding the mug because apparently confident and laidback Keaton knew nothing about how liquids worked when their container tipped sideways. Stupid Keaton knew it now as beer poured from mug to lap.

Back in the day, I'd been smooth, cool, a guy with moves. Now, I had autumn ale soaking through from denim to underwear. But I also had Avery just a few measly feet away, biting her lip to keep from laughing, failing, and a giggle bubbled out of her as she made her way toward me.

She crossed her arms. "I might not be the league MVP, so if this is a new way to consume beer, well done, but maybe you should consider rubber pants until you get the hang of it."

I could have said my dick was thirsty, but I smiled because the only thing I wanted to say was how good she looked, how much I wanted to sit at a quiet table with her and catch up. I was dying to tell her that the two weeks I spent with her were the best I'd ever had and more than anything, I wanted to apologize, to make things right between us.

Instead, I sat there smiling like a fool as another guy walked up, touched her on the shoulder, and said, "Susie got us a table. I'll get the drinks, what do you want?"

She glanced at him then back at me and waves of red rolled up her neck to her cheeks and I wondered if she was remembering the night she'd licked salt for her tequila shots off my neck, because I sure as hell was remembering.

She cleared her throat and smiled softly. "Just a…diet soda with lime."

He nodded and walked behind the bar as if he owned the place, and I remembered him, Alex something. Our bartender from college, his parents did actually own the place. Then it dawned on me, Alex was the boyfriend. I hated him, the lucky bastard.

I could've been that guy; if only I'd figured out a way to make her forgive me for making that fucking bet.

One Decade Ago

Ryder tossed his game controller on the couch.

"Fuck!"

I'd kicked his ass for about the tenth time this morning and gloating had lost most of its magic appeal. But I still took the money he bet me on each round of the game.

I shrugged and stood. "You can't play GTA, or Madden, and nobody is calling your ass for duty, maybe you should stick with ballet." Little known fact, but ballet helped with coordination and muscle strengthening, endurance, and balance. None of which Ryder would ever be praised for, but he protected me on the line and gave me time in the pocket and if ballet helped him do that, I'd suit up in my own leotard and plie right alongside him. But he hated that I knew about his dance class so, of course, I used it to my advantage. He wanted to go pro more than he was worried about what anyone thought, except me. It didn't make him less of an asshole though, and I didn't mind teasing him about it. "I bet you look hot in a tutu."

"Yeah well, your girl likes it when I take it off." His eyes narrowed, but I couldn't resist, much the same as he couldn't resist being an asshole.

The joke was on him, I didn't have a girl, not a steady one. "Look at it this way. You and your dates can share clothes."

He nodded, almost smiling, but with Ryder, that kind of facial flex meant something sinister was on its way.

"At least my dates can go out in the sun

without bursting into flames." So, he knew about my time with Avery. "You lose a bet or something?"

Actually, since I'd been hanging out with Avery, luck had been on my side. I'd been kicking ass at practice, couldn't throw an interception or an incomplete pass, but I kept it to myself. "You don't like her?"

"Like her? Fuck, no. Am I scared she's going to turn you into a toad if this all goes south? Yeah." He laughed. "Swear to God. If I see a single wart sprouting on you, I'm calling for an exorcism, no questions asked, I got your back, buddy."

What he had was a bunch of mixed-up ideas about vampires, witches, and Satanists. Apparently, he couldn't decide which classification fit her, and I didn't care to correct him. "Yeah. Thanks."

"Why are you wasting time with her anyway? I mean, first, you had Beth Cooper then that hot little peace and love hippie wanting a piece of your action. Now you're dating the dark side." He kicked his feet up on the coffee table and crossed his ankles. This was the most interest I'd ever seen Ryder take in a person whose panties he wasn't trying to get into. But something about him said he wasn't as disinterested as he seemed to want me to think.

"We're working on a project together." Not like I could tell him more than that without betraying Avery and I was curious to see how this all played out.

"Talk to the teacher. You can probably get out of it." Ryder used his status as an All-American football player to get out of anything he didn't want to do, mostly homework.

"Nah. I'm good." I hadn't expected to enjoy being with Avery as much as I did. But now, thinking about her made me smile.

He stared at me, and I looked away.

"You want her." He cocked an eyebrow like

he'd made some big revelation. "Dude. There are about a thousand girls at this school who'll be happy to polish your trophy without you having to get a tetanus shot and see a priest after. Molly Orman. Shala Hughes." He ticked off about five more names on his fingers before he narrowed his eyes. "Sigmas. Omegas. Kappas. You're Keaton Shaw, a legend, a phenom. Panties melt when you walk into a room. You don't need Vampira when there's an entire sack of sorority girls ready to scream your name into their pillows."

And there it was. He'd made the point I'd been ignoring, I wanted Avery. "She wants to be a Sigma."

"And I want a bigger dick." He looked down. "Of course, I already have to tie it down to keep it from peeking out over my jeans, so bigger might be overkill."

I rolled my eyes at his preoccupation with size. He had the biggest truck, the biggest room in the house, the biggest bank account and he made sure everyone knew it. Dick size was just another on his list.

He laughed and took a beer from the bucket next to the sofa. After he handed me one, he popped his open and took a long swig before he spoke again.

"There's no way she'll ever be a Sigma. Even if you can, and I doubt it, make her half-ass presentable, she doesn't have the money or status."

As I stared at my beer, rather than strangle him like I wanted to, he chuckled. "I mean, I'd probably do her so long as she doesn't bring out her spell book or try to soak me in her cauldron" He wiggled his eyebrows "but she isn't really the kind of girl that's going to fit in when we graduate and go pro."

Not something I hadn't considered already, but it wasn't as much about transforming her into a Sigma as it was about helping her...get Ryder. Shit. "Maybe."

And maybe I wanted to stop the whole

thing, except then I wouldn't have a reason to see her and that was unacceptable.

"You should just fuck her and get it over with so you can get back to being yourself." He laughed as if he'd just told the funniest joke ever spoken.

"She isn't like that." He stared at me until my skin burned. "She's…different."

"Different. What does that mean?" I didn't answer. I didn't tell him that she didn't want me and unfortunately, I didn't have to. But I also didn't tell him she *did* want him.

"Holy shit. You found the one girl in this whole fucking place that doesn't want to roll around naked with you." He laughed and clapped his hands together. "I might love her warts and all."

And I really didn't like him talking about her like that. "Fuck you, Ry."

He laughed again. "You might as well do me. Since you aren't gonna be getting any of that." He was about ten seconds from getting his ass kicked outside the video game and then he went in for the kill. "I bet you ten crisp new Benjamins you don't even get to third base and another ten the Sigmas won't take her either."

Stupidest move I'd ever made was taking his bet.

Chapter 7

Avery

But for my lie, this wouldn't have been one of the most awkward moments of my life. Now though, with Keaton on one side and Alex on the other with Susie across from me, it ranked at least the top three, especially with the intensity of Susie's glare at Keaton.

I turned to my best friend, the one who hadn't told me about his relationship with Susie.

"Hey, hon." Susie's gaze snapped from

Keaton to me when I spoke so softly and sweetly to Alex. "Why don't you go get us another drink?"

Alex blinked twice as though my words didn't quite register. In fairness, I never, in all our years as friends, used an endearment, especially one with such an intimate connotation, come to think of it, I couldn't remember a time with anyone else either.

"Sure." He stood and held his hand out to Susie. "Come along?"

She slipped her palm over his and laced their fingers together, then she cocked an eyebrow at me. A challenge? A dare? A warning? I didn't really care since my interest in Alex was purely fictional. Still, it would've been nice if he'd given me a bit of warning so I could've explained my need to him and he could've rebuffed me in enough time I could've hired a date so I didn't look so laughable now. Of course, had I not been forced to detail my devious plot to his voicemail, this moment might've been a little less…humiliating.

Keaton watched me until they were gone. "That's not your boyfriend."

My skin heated, I could have lied but looking more foolish than I already did seemed a bit of overkill. "No."

He nodded. "I don't have one either."

Okay, I'd been busted for lying. I could live with that. "Well, I'm sure if you had a boyfriend, I would've read about it. Since I've read about every girlfriend you've had since college."

His grin made my heart wobble, and I put a hand over my chest trying to still it from the outside. As if.

"You read about me?"

Heat flashed through me. There wasn't much I could do to save myself now. In for a penny… "Yeah. I read about your sixty-seven percent passer rating, sixteen interceptions, and forty-one sacks last year. I assume that's why you're here and not there."

He took the barb and shrugged while using his thumbnail to scrape the label from his beer bottle.

"I'm on the concussion list." He didn't look up. "I think they're going to release me."

"Oh shit." I covered his hand with mine. "I'm sorry. I know how much football means to you." He smiled still gazing at his beer bottle.

"I could tell you something horrible about me, so you can poke fun."

"That might help." He said with a humble chuckle.

"I got kicked out of a Bon Jovi concert," I said quickly, bluntly, and with a little shame.

He chuckled. "Is the part that bothers you that you got kicked out or that you went to see Bon Jovi in the first place?"

"See? You feel better already, don't you?" I liked his smile, loved his laugh, actually, sat in the bar picturing myself curling up against him.

"I do. Thank you." He laid his hand over

mine and stroked my fingers with his thumb. "You have that magical effect."

I wanted him to keep touching me, but for the life of me, I couldn't think of how to make that happen. "Me and football."

"Well, I guess it's just you now." His life hadn't been all peaches and ice cream before college. His mom suffered from some sort of mental illness, his dad was a workaholic and his brother died in Afghanistan. Football was Keaton's escape. "It is what it is." But it wasn't. The hurt and fear in his eyes spoke louder than his lie.

I'd watched every game he played, even paid extra for the sports pack so I wouldn't miss a single interview, although he sounded better in person than through my television. More than anything in my life that I'd ever wanted, I wanted to wipe that frown off his face. "I still remember you trying to teach me to throw a football. I was so bad at it."

Finally, he looked up and the smile was back. "Not so bad."

What I remembered most was the way his body pressed into mine as he stood behind me, the way his arms came around me, and his hand laid over the top of mine as he lined my fingers with the laces. That was the moment things changed for me.

One Decade Ago

I didn't walk past the Alpha house very often. It wasn't on my way home or way to class, but today, I wanted to see if they'd managed to paint over Susie's handiwork yet. She'd gotten creative last night and she and her crew had drawn various sized penises on the brick. And this time, she'd expanded her portfolio to include the side of the house. She'd said it was too easy for them to just keep covering her insults and she'd wanted a bigger canvas.

One Bet

As expected, they had their pledges outside, paintbrushes locked and loaded, adult cloth diapers on, while Keaton threw a football back and forth with Finn Makenzie, another Alpha. Finn threw high, Keaton jumped, and I caught the ball, dropping my bag of books and papers. I held the ball as Keaton jogged toward me.

"You know, for being such a hotshot football player, you kind of suck."

He grinned and picked up my bag. "I'm a quarterback, not a receiver." We exchanged the ball for the bag, and he hugged it like a teenage girl that wasn't me would hug her favorite teddy bear. For a second, just the one, I stared at the way he cradled the ball, and a little ball of jealousy hardened in my stomach. I wanted to be that football. "You want to play?"

"I don't think so. I'm more of a baseball kind of girl." I hadn't walked by to end up embarrassing myself. These guys were gonna be pros someday, and my skills hadn't been tested since I'd forced the county to let me play peewee football in grade school.

"Come on." He relieved me of my bag again, then handed me the ball. "Go on. I'll help you throw it to Finn and you'll see how easy it is."

Part of the reason I dressed the way I did was to discourage my inclusion in group activities, like playing catch with a football in the front yard of a fraternity house. Besides, if Ryder saw me being a pathetic non-athlete, what would he think?

That thought lasted all of one second, right up to the moment Keaton moved behind me and slid his hands from my shoulders to my wrists. He lowered one to my side then used it to angle our hips, so we were no longer facing Finn head-on. "You hold the ball like this." His voice was thick and low as he moved my fingers with his to rest between the laces on the ball. His touch sent electricity zinging along my cells and his voice made my panties start to melt.

Every other thing about him made my entire body go hot. And how had I not noticed how good Keaton smelled? Woodsy with a hint of spice, I shivered but stayed put. I couldn't have moved if a sudden hurricane ate the shoreline away and barreled toward me. My palms grew damp, my heart kicked up a few paces, my stomach clenched and I liked all of it.

He stepped back. "All right. Now cock your arm back." He demonstrated without touching me, and the muscle in his biceps contracted into a ball of pure sexy. "When you bring it forward, release when you get to right here." He used his arm to demonstrate. "Ready?"

I aimed for Finn with my mind more than my hand and my arm. Before I could pull it forward, Keaton stepped in again and this time, his breath warmed my ear as his arm wrapped around my waist so his free hand could rest on my belly. Damn.

"Not so far. And don't concentrate so hard. You're just playing a game of catch."

He might as well have whispered something decadent and naughty for all the focus I had on throwing the damned ball. All I could think about was Keaton whispering something decadent and naughty as his thumb rubbed small lines on my belly. His chest pressed against my back, his mouth curled next to my skin.

"Hey! Are you two gonna make out or throw the ball?" Finn stood across the yard, hands on his hips.

I did the only thing I could think to do. I took a step out of Keaton's grasp and let fly with a spiral. I might've already known how to throw a football that hit him square in the numbers. He caught the ball with sure hands and laughed. "She might be trying out for your job next year, Shaw."

Keaton moved behind me again. "I think you hustled me."

One Bet

"I never said I couldn't throw a ball." My voice cracked and my skin felt alive like it had its own wattage and it was because of him. Shit, this wasn't supposed to be happening. I wasn't supposed to be attracted to Keaton, it was supposed to be Ryder that made my heart pitter-patter and my panties get wet. Ryder Kennedy not Keaton Shaw, but damn, Keaton felt nice. I chuckled through my confusion. "Fair warning. Just don't ever bet on pool with me."

I turned, and we were chest to chest. "You'll go home broke and sad."

And if his chest felt nice against my back, it was pure heaven against my chest. Holy shit, I wanted Keaton. Now. On the lawn, in the car, anywhere I could get him.

"I never get sad over money."

"That's because you have a lot of it." I didn't mean to say it. The last thing I wanted right then was to point out the differences between us, especially when I could see all the shades of blue in his eyes, but once again, my mouth let me down. And now I wanted to get out of there before I said something else stupid, but I also wanted to stay right there, with his arms around me and those big blue eyes pointed at mine. "I should go."

"Okay." He stepped back and cleared his throat. I looked across the yard as the football came sailing at Keaton again. This time, I blocked the blow and the ball sailed left.

But he laughed and chased the ball, even his slight jog inspired fantasies of sex, especially when he bent down to pick up the ball then stood, turned toward me, and grinned. "You want to come to protect me in the pocket, too?"

A flirty girl could have run ten miles with that sentence, but I just smiled. "Somebody should." I shook my head. "I have to go. Homework tonight?"

"Yeah. I'll meet you at the library after practice, around seven?"

One Bet

I nodded and left. Not one time on the way home did I think of Ryder.

Chapter 8

Keaton

Seeing her again was like a punch in my gut. It knocked the wind out of me every time and her smile lit the whole place up. She'd changed her hair from the platinum we'd colored it to in college to a darker, softer blonde, and she'd traded the fishnets and cardigans in for a Glouster hoodie and jeans that hugged her ass and waist. She'd grown some new curves since college, and I really liked them. More with each beer I drank and each memory that came crashing back.

When she left with Susie to go to the bathroom, I realized I loved watching her walk and talk and smile. All those old feelings came flooding back, and I was powerless to stop myself from wanting her. Or maybe I didn't want to stop myself. Being with her had made me happy back then. And it had been such a long time since I'd been happy. But it didn't matter, she'd kept a wall built between us and I couldn't blame her. I only wished her friend had the same respect for boundaries.

He'd been moving his chair closer as the bar filled up with more alumni and current coeds. Hero worship was usually one of my favorite things in life, but now I just wanted him to go away. Every question and comment reminded me of my failed career, my failed life. "Do you know when you'll be back to playing?"

I shook my head. "No."

I didn't tell him it depended on the scans I'd

so far refused to get. Some of the information, strangers didn't need to know, no matter how much they pushed.

"That game last year against Atlanta, that Hail Mary you threw to end the game, it was brilliant."

It was luck; I hadn't even been able to see the ball by the time I had to lob the ball down the field.

From behind me, I heard the squeal before I saw the woman. "Keaton Shaw!"

Oh no. I knew that voice, and she wasn't someone I wanted to see while I was with Avery. I was fairly certain Avery wouldn't want to see her either, but short of sprinting in the other direction, there wasn't much I could do.

She shuffled over, literally, slid on her heels in that excited way girls did with arms wide and chest barreling straight toward me. Her implants poked my pecs as she leaned down to squeeze me.

"Hey, Beth." Once a Sigma, always a

Sigma. At least that was what the sash she wore said, Beth Cooper had been the ultimate sorority girl. A legacy who'd walked right into the house and became its queen. And now she was a talk show host who'd offered to bring her entire crew to shoot the homecoming festivities that would culminate in next Saturday's big game. Of course, Glouster's regents had snapped up that offer. Anything to increase the student population. And publicity like the Beth Cooper Show didn't come around every day.

"Oh my God, you look amazing." She ran her hands over my shoulders and down my chest. "I've missed you."

We'd dated for about one minute in college because until I'd met Avery only one girl had lasted longer than a few minutes, and that girl hated me now, although I didn't know why and after Avery, no one measured up. Beth wasn't bad, she just wasn't the *one*. Not that it was her fault, from the first time I talked to her, something about Avery dimmed the light of every other woman I knew.

"It's great to see you, too." After all these years, Beth still dressed in the college coed on the prowl uniform of short skirt and tight top to accent the curves she maintained with pilates and yoga. She wore just enough makeup to highlight and enhance, and she smiled her signature smile, the toothy, perfectly lined grin that all the cameras loved.

Her eyes went wide. "Oh my God. I just had a brilliant idea. You should come to my show. I could get a whole new demographic. Men, who like sports, like football." She shook her head at each pause in her words. "Let's set that up."

I nodded. "Sure. Just get a hold of my agent, she can work it around my schedule." Which lately had a lot of openings.

And as soon as I left, I would be calling Olivia and advising her not to set up anything. Beth Cooper didn't do sports, never had. She did fashion and high society, she did formal dances and fundraisers and none of those things were bad. They just weren't something I could sit on the sofa and pretend to enjoy.

She stood to her full height and looked over my shoulder, her bright white smile faded.

"Really, Keaton? Her again?" She crossed her arms. "You didn't learn when she got Ryder and Finn and the other one kicked out of school? When she wrote that article?"

Maybe my reaction time had slowed as much as my brain function, but Beth shoved me out of the way and stomped around the table to stand in front of Avery before it occurred to me to stop her. "I can't believe you have the nerve to show your face after what you did."

Oh shit, I tugged on Beth's arm but she jerked away hard and caught Avery in the right cheek with her balled-up fist. Avery's head jerked then she came back around, fire dancing in her eyes and blood pouring from a cut in her cheek from Beth's college ring. I moved between them to shield Avery with my body. "Beth…what the fuck?"

"Get out of the way, Keaton. That felt good and I think I want to do it again." She tried to veer around me, but I shifted. I couldn't see Avery, but I could feel her anger. I also didn't know if she would battle it out with fists or not, but I didn't trust Beth not to go after Avery's job if Avery did happen to fight back.

"You're 32 fucking years old, Beth and she can kick your ass. Walk away before you do something you regret." And then I remembered the real reason Beth and I didn't work out.

One Decade Ago

My phone vibrated for the tenth time, Avery glanced from it to me and I picked it up to shove it into my pocket. "You can answer it."

"It's no big deal." And I meant it. "Not important."

She smiled and sat back, arms crossed, eyes narrowed. "Yes, unimportant things call ten times in an hour."

"I kind of forgot a date I'm supposed to be on." Why did I tell her? I hadn't planned to, but she short-circuited all my systems enough I couldn't control my mouth or much else. She closed her book then reached for mine and flipped the cover closed. "You should go."

"It's no big deal." Not to me, but I had a suspicion Beth Cooper felt quite differently. Had this date not been arranged last week when the Sigma girls had arranged a mixed bowling night and Beth put our names down, I wouldn't have forgotten it, or maybe it was Avery that made me forget. Well, not Avery exactly, but the fact I wanted to be with her more than I wanted to go bowling with the Sigmas.

The phone vibrated again.

"You should definitely go." She shoved her

books into her bag and stood before the ringing even stopped. "I'll see you tomorrow."

She pushed around the table and almost jogged to the door.

By the time I gathered my stuff, shoved it into my backpack, and caught up with her, she was already out the door and halfway down the sidewalk. "Avery, wait."

She sniffed and turned, but it was more like she flung her body in a half-circle to stare at me. And oh no. She was crying.

"Avery, what's wrong?" She shook her head and resumed walking. This time, she went in the other direction. I stepped in front of her. "Tell me."

She shook her head then ran her fingers through her short hair making it stand up on top. I would've described her as adorably disheveled and sad. "I don't know, okay? I just…I don't know." She swerved around me and started walking again. "It's the stupidest thing and I don't understand it."

One Bet

Something inside me broke when she sniffed again. "Hey. It's okay. Whatever it is you can tell me, we're friends, you can tell me *anything*." I just wanted her to be okay. Even if she said she hated me and never wanted to see me again. Well, that might've been a lie, but I wanted to be the kind of man who said it as truth, that had to count for something.

"We're not friends, Keaton. The only reason we're here is that you need better grades, and I wanted to go out with Ryder."

Wanted to, past tense, my heart kicked up its pace. This time, I took her hand and stopped walking, tugged when she kept going. I had no idea what I was doing. I only knew I wanted to do it more than anything in the world.

When she turned to face me, I gave her fingers a squeeze. "That's the reason we were in there. Not why we're out here." I moved closer, still holding onto her hand.

"You have a date." She swallowed hard as I lifted my free hand to her cheek, to brush my thumb over her lips. I'd been dying to touch her since I first walked into the library and saw her smiling as she read some book she hid as soon as she saw me.

"I'd rather be with you." And just as I lowered my head to kiss her, a car screeched to a stop beside us. Beth Cooper had impeccably bad timing.

"What the actual fuck are you doing with *her* when you're supposed to be on a date with me?" Her shriek echoed off the building around us as she climbed out of her little red coupe and stomped to the sidewalk, bowling shoes flapping on the concrete with each step.

I dropped my hands and stared at Beth as if I'd never seen her before and honestly, I hadn't, not this side of her anyway.

"Beth, we were studying." Of course, that didn't explain why I'd been about to kiss Avery, and saying it like that was wrong on so many levels when I had certainly been about to kiss her.

"She's trash, Keaton, the little charity case doesn't belong here, she belongs at a community college." I'd never heard such venom come out of another person's mouth, and maybe the surprise of it was why I didn't spring to Avery's defense, or maybe it was the fact I expected Avery to jump in and kill Beth, but instead, she nodded next to me, smiled and walked away. Shamefully, I didn't stop her or go after her, I just stood there like an asshole and let her go.

Chapter 9

Avery

Four stitches, on my face, didn't that just figure? Keaton was back in town one day, and all of a sudden, I had a facial laceration.

He sat on a chair in the exam room as the doctor finished sewing me up. "If you want to go...," I'd been embarrassed before, a lot of times, but I'd never been kicked out of a bar for fighting, getting my ass kicked on accident, or ended up in an emergency room after a bar fight.

He cocked his head and stared with his mouth in a half frown, half-smile and I waited until the doctor walked out of the room before I could think of anything else to say. "Don't you have to get back to the frat house?"

He continued staring. "I'm staying at a hotel in Brighton."

If this day could get worse, I wasn't sure how. "Okay."

"Are you going to be in trouble at work?"

Oh, well now I knew how it could get worse. A bar fight wasn't expected or acceptable behavior for a professor at Glouster University. Although it wasn't spelled out in the handbook as more than *an obligation to maintain upstanding behavior consistent with Glouster's values*, I was fairly certain a bar fight might violate my contract.

"I don't know." Of course, I would be in trouble, Beth Cooper was an alumnus revered by the regents for her successes. She was the pride of the school, right behind Keaton. Not for the first time, it occurred to me that the cosmos probably had it in for me because I'd gone above and beyond to keep the pretty people apart.

"She attacked you." He shrugged. "There are probably twenty videos…" He paused, and I would have thought he forgot his train of thought if I didn't know exactly what it was he was thinking of.

I chuckled at the absurdity of this whole thing. "Wow. You know how to make a bad day really bad."

But what happened a decade ago couldn't hurt me anymore, even if the video had somehow managed to survive the test of time.

And his smile was as potent as ever when he aimed it at me, my heart did a quick thump-thump as the nurse whipped back the curtain to hand me a set of discharge papers. She tilted my head and surveyed the doctor's work.

"Make an appointment for six days with your regular doctor, he can take those out for you." She tilted my head further. "You might have a little scar, but he did good stitches, so I think you'll be pleased with the result. You can take some over-the-counter pain relief if you need it."

I nodded and hopped off the gurney as Keaton stood. "Okay. Thanks."

As we walked out, I kept my head down. I made it to the door and waited for Keaton who'd been held up by a nurse who wanted his autograph. She snuck in a selfie, and I laughed as he shrugged. When he joined me outside, he dropped his hand to the small of my back and guided me toward the parking lot.

"Are you okay to drive if I take you back to your car or do you want me to take you to Brighton?"

Since he'd been drinking beer and I'd stuck to soda, I'd driven to the hospital. I would've happily come alone, but he insisted and hopped into the car before I thought to hit the lock button. "Do you have anyone to stay with you tonight?"

I chuckled. "It's four stitches. I didn't hit my head or blackout. I think I'll be okay."

But a little part of me poked her hopeful little head up and smiled that he wanted to stay.

"You're always okay." He shoved his hands into his pockets and leaned his back against my driver's door. "I always admired that about you."

If he knew me at all, he would've known that I was hardly ever okay. I was just good at pretending. And thank God for it. "Everything isn't always what it looks like, Keaton."

I could have told him stories that would make his hair curl. Especially after everything that went down senior year.

"I always thought it was with you. You want something, you figure out how to get it. I spent so much time sitting on my hands and not doing anything. But you...," He shook his head. "You get what you want."

And I shouldn't have asked. I knew it as soon as I spoke that I shouldn't have. "What do you want?"

Long seconds passed, might have been minutes, before he pushed off the car and stood in front of me. His fingers threaded through my hair and he leaned in, slow, steady, gaze never leaving mine right up to the minute my eyelids fluttered shut and his kiss transported me back to another time and place.

One Decade Ago

Trash, charity case, the words rang through my head as I walked home. During my bath and when I curled up in my bed and tried to sleep. When I closed my eyes, I saw Keaton standing on the sidewalk telling her we were *just studying*. Somehow, I'd convinced my stupid self that it was more. Fuck, I was stupid.

This whole thing had spun out of my control, I wasn't supposed to like Keaton. I wanted Ryder. Since I first walked onto campus and saw him. But Ryder didn't have icy blue eyes that made me want to melt when he looked at me, he didn't smell like cinnamon and spice and his hand didn't fit at the small of my back. Well, it might've but I wouldn't know because he'd never looked at me, never touched me, never spoken to me and now, he wasn't the one whose hands I wanted on my skin.

My tiny apartment was nothing more than one room and a bathroom over a garage that belonged to the Glouster University chaplain and his family. But it was my space, and if I wanted to cry my eyes out here, at least I didn't have a roommate to watch me do it. Of course, I didn't have a roommate to commiserate with or cry to or to keep me from checking my phone 79 times because I hoped he would call and reassure me that her words were hers and not his. That he didn't care how Beth Cooper felt, that I wasn't trash.

Around midnight, I sat up and walked to the mini-fridge. If I couldn't sleep, I could at least eat a bowl of cereal and maybe skip breakfast in the morning. My dishes, two bowls, two plates, a pot, and a skillet, were on shelves lined over the small sink that doubled as a food prep area thanks to the board that usually laid on top. I pulled down a bowl and poured from a box of Cap'n Crunch, added milk, and took a spoon from the single drawer in the "kitchen."

As I walked the three steps from the sink to the bed, someone knocked on the door. Since it didn't happen very often, I jumped, sloshing cereal and milk down the front of me. "Shit."

But I reached to twist the knob as I set the bowl on the dresser and used my now free hand to brush the streams of milk from my shirt. And it was his voice that made me look up. "Hey."

Keaton stood in the doorway, hair mussed, hands in his pockets. "What are you doing here?"

"I'm sorry." His voice was soft, pained. "So sorry."

I couldn't fault him for being who he was, much the same as I couldn't fault me for being who I was. It was just sad that the me I was wasn't good enough for the him he was. "Okay."

I turned away and brought my cereal back to the sink then used the towel I kept for dish drying to dry the front of my shirt. Looking at him hurt me. Made Beth Cooper's words louder in my head. *Trash, charity case,* bitch.

When I turned, he hadn't moved from the doorway. "Avery, please."

I looked at him because something in his voice made me want to see his face. His lids lowered, and he held out his hand. Going to him meant setting myself up to be hurt, but standing so far away caused a deeper ache, worse than anything I could have imagined. I walked close enough to put my hand over his and made the decision to pull him inside.

He came in, kicked the door shut, closed the distance between us, and wrapped one arm around my waist. His other hand wrapped around the back of my neck and nudged me closer with his fingertips. "I should've done this a long time ago."

I smiled. "We've only known each other a couple days."

He shook his head. "I feel like I've known you forever."

Then he lowered his head and brushed his lips over mine. My heart pounded against my ribs, and I didn't care if he felt it, I wanted him to know it was for him, all him.

He deepened the kiss, used his tongue to trace the seam of my lips, and I opened my mouth. Dear God this man knew how to kiss. It made me want so much more. Right up to the minute he pulled away and leaned his forehead against mine.

My breath came in short bursts, and I closed my eyes because looking at him wasn't going to help me calm down. Neither would, "Can I kiss you again?"

But I nodded anyway. Even let him walk me back to the bed and lower me to the mattress, all the while kissing me and massaging my scalp with his fingertips. I wanted him so badly it scared me. It made me pull away. I'd never even been on a real date, and I'd damned sure never gone further than second base.

"Keaton."

Instead of kissing me again, he rolled onto his back and gathered me next to him. I could hear his heartbeat under my cheek, and it lulled me enough to close my eyes and fall asleep on his chest.

Chapter 10

Keaton

With my career in ruins, my history with Avery murky and clouded by a kiss I practically forced on her, I woke up hungover and hopeless. I shouldn't have come back. If I hadn't, Avery's job wouldn't be at risk.

There had to be something I could do to fix this. Even if my career was circling the drain, at least I could use what was left of my reputation on campus for some good. The thought inspired me. Once upon a time, I'd destroyed any hope for me and Avery, but now, I had the chance to make at least one thing right.

I rushed through a shower, down to the garage, and only then remembered I'd left my car at Hilly's. Thank God for Lyft. As I waited for the car service to arrive, I made my plan.

"Hey. That game last year against Los Angeles?" The driver stared at me through his rearview. He had dark curly hair and aviator shades, but I couldn't shake the notion that I knew him, maybe it was the voice. "Your offensive line let you down, man."

The truth was, I didn't even remember most of that game. I'd been sacked in the first quarter and spent the rest of the game just trying to see straight. I'd been so desperate to stay in the game, to not be replaced by the younger, stronger rookie, that I'd almost killed myself trying to finish strong. We'd lost by two touchdowns.

"It takes a whole team to win or lose." But it

had been me and my selfish play, my fear of being replaced that had lost that game and a bunch of others.

"Yeah, but they gotta protect you. When you aren't safe in the pocket, you can't throw a pass. It's football science." He chuckled. "Not rocket science."

He sounded like our college line coach. Exactly like our college line coach. "Do I know you?"

"Blew out my knee senior year." He glanced at me again and tipped down his shades. "How you been, Keats?"

"King?" Jameson King had been a fraternity brother until the Alabama game when our world was already on a path to implosion and he'd gone down and never come back up. He'd been an All-Star wide receiver who could outrun a cheetah. And he'd had offers from three pro teams. I'd been so busy making a name for myself, I'd forgotten about him. I might've recognized him though had he not been wearing those damned shades and sitting in the front seat while I sat in the back.

"Yeah." He nodded. "You got the contract, I got three surgeries and a chauffer's license." The bitterness in his voice jabbed at the secret I'd kept from everyone, made me want to share it with an old friend.

But I wouldn't insult him by telling him how great my contract wasn't, how I couldn't remember my own name sometimes, or how my vision clouded enough I once drove through a stop sign….not the intersection, the actual sign. "I'm sorry, Jameson."

"It's good. I got a wife, three kids, a dog, could've been worse." His voice was low, laced with disappointment, probably for what could've been had we not fallen apart.

But if I was honest, his life sounded pretty great to me. "That's great."

He pulled a picture off his dashboard and handed it over the seat to me. "That's Susie. You remember her? Ryder…"

Oh shit. Yeah, I remembered her. From *last night*. "And these are your kids?"

He laughed. "Yeah. Her red hair. My curls." He nodded but didn't look at me. "We were friends before…everything happened and she came to the hospital every day after I got hurt."

It was funny the things I couldn't remember versus what I could. "You brought her home after that night." She'd walked out of the bedroom, upset and crying. Finn and I had been in the kitchen when we heard the video, but someone shut it off before I got into the living room. A couple of the guys had laughed, but Jameson had followed her out.

"Yeah. Ryder was always an asshole." He chuckled. "But then again, we all were."

And we weren't the only ones. His wife seemed to have some explaining to do. Bro code said I should tell him, but he pulled into the lot at Hilly's and shoved the car into park. "You should come to dinner while you're in town. Susie makes a mean meatloaf."

Well, wouldn't that just be awkward as hell? But he'd been a good friend once and he'd saved my ass. One awkward dinner wasn't too much to ask, I owed him that much. "Yeah. Sounds good. Can I bring a date?"

If Avery ever wanted to see me again, I thought she might like to see how this played out.

He nodded and chuckled. "Yeah. How about Friday night? After the alumni mixer?"

"Great. Sounds great." More than anything, I wanted to call Avery and ask her to come with me, I also wanted to tell her what I knew. I wondered if her number was still the same.

One Decade Ago

I drove back to the frat house with the biggest smile I'd ever felt on my face. For not having screwed her, I'd never been so happy to just *sleep* with someone, as a matter of fact, I never had. At least not since I fell asleep with Lydia Marks in ninth grade when she came to visit me after I got my first concussion at football practice.

That smile carried me through right up to the minute she saw me in a film studies class, and she sat across the room from me. *Across the room*. Certainly not the reaction I expected from someone who folded herself into my side and laid her head on my shoulder while I watched her eyelids flutter and her soft slow smiles while she dreamed.

And I wasn't about to let this go. I picked up my stuff and moved to sit beside her. She countered by returning to the seat I'd vacated. Professor Weller watched us as I followed her again, but I didn't care.

"Don't be the guy I have to get a restraining order against." She hissed the words at me, and Professor Weller cleared his throat and shot us a glare as Audrey Hepburn and Rex

Harrison sang some ridiculous song on the projection screen.

What the hell happened? Three hours ago, she was cuddled up next to me with her arm over my stomach and her knee curled over mine, three hours ago.

"Avery, what's going on?" My unfortunate timing of a silent part in the video made my question sound a lot louder than I'd meant it to be.

Professor Weller paused the video. "Could you two kindly take this outside?"

Avery huffed out a loud breath and gathered her stuff then stomped to the front of the class and out the door, I followed because no way could I let it go at this.

She walked a few steps ahead then turned around to face me. "Look, Keaton, this was a bad idea, a mistake." Her skin shaded a dusky red, but she turned to walk away again and because I was pathetic for her, I followed.

"Please, Avery. Talk to me." She stopped and sighed as if I was truly bothering her.

She opened her mouth, snapped it shut, then opened it again. "No."

"What did I do?" For the first time in my life, I actually felt a pain in my heart. Over a girl and to be clear, it was a girl I'd only known a couple of days.

She sighed and pursed her lips. I hoped it meant she was going to tell me, but she shook her head again and kept walking. After a minute she came back as she simultaneously dug around in her purse then handed me her cell phone. "Put your phone number in here."

"Okay." I took the phone, hoping this was a good sign. When I handed it back, she turned again, and this time, jogged off into the distance.

A minute later, my cell pinged.

You have more experience than I do.

I stared at the words until I realized what she meant. Then I smiled.

Is that a problem?

Clearly, it was for her, but it also explained why she'd acted like I'd given her a disease, she was embarrassed. I pictured her, skin ruddy as she chewed her lower lip.

I don't even know how to sext.

That she'd thought about being with me as something other than a friend warmed my gut and made my dick twitch as another text came in.

I looked it up this morning before I realized I didn't have your number. But I could never say those things.

Relief swept through me, mingling with the desire to see her. I needed to save this moment. I needed to save whatever was becoming of us.

Avery, we don't have to sext. Or even have sex. I just want to get to know you. Can I see you tonight?

It took five solid minutes, minutes I spent staring at my phone, for her to reply.

You can see me now. Walk around the side of the building.

Those awkward, heartbreaking minutes I'd just survived were all worth it when I turned the corner and she pushed me back against the brick and made this the best morning after nothing happened that I'd ever had.

Chapter 11

Avery

I'd never even been called into the principal's office, but now sat, face bandaged, hands shaking, across the desk from the director of my department because a meeting had been called to discuss my conduct.

"Miss Stroh." He turned his computer to face me. "Is that you?"

I watched the video, it was after I'd been punched, and blood was trickling down my cheek. Beth Cooper stood screaming words I'd ignored and hadn't even remembered until I saw the video thanks to a bout of shock. "Yes."

"Had you been drinking?"

I hadn't, but it was none of his damned business. My behavior had been nothing but *consistent with Glouster's values*. I twisted the computer back to face him. "As you can see in the video, I did *not* react to this person's assault, nor did I do anything to earn it, I don't understand why I'm here."

He held up one finger as his phone rang, after a moment, he spoke. "I'm in a meeting with Miss Stroh." He paused and nodded. "Yes. I'll be right there." He hung up and glanced at me as he straightened his tie then slid his arms into the jacket he'd pulled from the back of his chair. "Excuse me for a moment."

I waited for twenty minutes for his return before I stood to pace behind my chair. He had a picture of himself with the cast of Friends and another with his arm around Beth Cooper in front of the BC logo on her talk show set.

Now I understood Beth Cooper, of course. With my luck, she was probably his daughter. Which meant I would lose my office, my class schedule, my paycheck. As I lamented my probable losses, he swung the door open and stood just inside. "Thank you for your time, Miss Stroh. I believe you have a class starting in ten minutes. You'd better hurry."

What? Not that I was complaining, but what? "Um, yes. I do."

I stood and smoothed down my lucky pencil skirt, its record was still undefeated and I didn't want to stick around to let him change his mind so I raced toward my modern film class.

And I would have walked in on time had Keaton not been waiting for me outside the door. "Hi."

"Hi." Last night's kiss was still fresh in my

mind, and I covered my mouth, hoping I could stop the memory from making me act foolishly.

"I guess everything went okay?"

How did he know there was an issue? "Yeah."

"Good." He nodded. "You have class now?"

He looked almost shy as he stood with his shoulder against the wall and his arms crossed and I was so pathetic I wanted to ditch my class and spend the afternoon ogling him.

"You want to sit in? We're talking about similarities and differences between modern and original cinema."

He chuckled. "I wish I could. I told the football coach I'd drop in on practice. Maybe you could text me later? We could…get dinner?"

He probably would've laughed if I told him I still had the phone I'd used to text him for the first time all those years ago and if I charged it, it would still have those same conversations in its memory. Not like I'd forgotten them either.

One Decade Ago

Decisions, decisions. We'd maintained a pretty steady and extremely innocent text conversation through our classes then skipped a few hours while he was at practice. Now though, I was seeking advice from a friend. I'd already sent Alex the requisite help-me text and when he didn't answer, I opened the app again and typed.

I want to send him something sexy, just to let him know I'm really interested, but I'm nervous.

The three little dots on my phone blinked. Ordinarily, I wouldn't ask for help. Especially not from Alex and most especially not for something like this. The amount of time it was taking him to reply did nothing to help my anxiety.

Why?

Ten minutes for that? Where was the friendship?

Because I'm not that kind of girl. I wouldn't even know what would turn him on.

Just try. I ignored the fact he'd never been so pushy before because I had asked for his help.

And it took a few minutes of staring at the phone and trying to remember what I'd read online before I finally typed and hit send quickly so I wouldn't chicken out. Even though it was only to Alex, it felt deeply personal and naughtier than I was used to. **Just laying here touching myself while I think about you.**

The little dots blinked again. **Really?**

Alex and I were friends….had been friends, would hopefully always be friends, but I wasn't giving him that kind of information, or maybe he meant *really* like it was a poor attempt at sexting. **Too much?**

I chewed my nail, but the text came back quickly. **Hell no. Tell me more.**

Alex! And it was then that I looked at the top of the screen and saw Keaton's name instead of Alex's.

Damn. I must've switched over after I asked Alex for help and not switched back. A quick look through the texts confirmed my stupidity. My skin caught fire and I couldn't breathe. The three dots flashed. Then stopped. Then flashed again.

Not Alex.

Not the revelation he probably thought, although the absolute confirmation made my stomach churn. Oh shit, I tossed the phone on the bed and pulled a pillow over my face. If it ever pinged again, I didn't want to know. But it did, and I couldn't *not* look.

Please don't tell me if it's not true.

My heart leaped and I wanted to be flirty and cool. There had to be something I could say that wouldn't give me away as a phony. I thought and thought before I came up with... **Wouldn't you like to know?** My finger hovered for a while before I hit send.

The reply came immediately. **Fuck yes. I would love to know.**

Keaton Shaw made everything so easy, this was just another thing I added to the list of things to like about him.

Chapter 12

Keaton

I watched the talent on the field and my stomach clenched, no way would I stay relevant in a league that had this caliber of up-and-coming rookies. But even with my sad realization, something about this place, this stadium comforted me, here I was a hero, a superstar. Once upon a time, I'd worn the red and black uniform, thrown the winning pass, brought home a championship.

Coach Rollins nodded to me as he watched

his players finishing up a scrimmage. The clock wound down and the horn sounded before he took off his headset and held out his hand to me. "Keaton Shaw."

Some things never changed. Not the bruising grip of his handshake, the booming vibrancy of his voice, the command to the team to huddle up and have a talk after practice.

After they all hashed out the problems they needed to work on, the strengths they had, and the changes that would be made, Rollins motioned for everyone to look at me.

"You all know Keaton Shaw. Best quarterback Glouster's ever seen." His ringing endorsement didn't include my pro stats, thank goodness. My glory days ended the minute I signed that contract, and I really didn't need the playback of my less-than-stellar performance. *Performances.*

For the next several minutes, they worshipped me with praise and hand slaps, high fives, and fist bumps. "It takes a team."

I'd expected the coach to agree, but he looked at the guys. "A team with good leadership and instincts. Keaton had that, on and off the field."

On the field, maybe. Off the field…not so much. Not always.

He sent the team to the showers, then motioned for me to walk beside him to his office. When we entered, he handed me a beer and I sat across from him. "What's the doctor say?"

I hadn't told anyone, not even my mom, but I wanted to tell Rollins. He would understand. Still, saying the words made my temple throb. "Another concussion and I could end up…" I shook my head. "In a wheelchair, bed-ridden, dead."

"Who knows?"

"You. Me. Olivia."

He smiled at the mention of my agent. "Now there's a woman who knows her business." I nodded because he was right and

One Bet

because no one argued with Coach Rollins. I wasn't about to be the first. "She can talk football with any man, at any time."

I nodded, she also worked the best deals and was the reason I hadn't been cut from the team yet. "Yeah. I owe her. A lot."

He shook off whatever he was thinking with an actual head shake then folded his hands on top of his desk. "Did you ever get your degree?"

I'd signed before the end of my senior year and took incompletes for my classes. "No."

He shrugged and stared at me. "Look, kid, I need a good quarterback coach. You can't teach instinct, but you can show them when to use it and how to look up the field. How to find the receiver, when to run, when to cover up. You interested?" When I didn't answer right away, he cocked his head. "It's a pay cut, but it keeps you in the game."

Football had been my everything from the time I first learned to throw a ball. The game had seen me through a childhood that could've broken me, gave me discipline and a life I could've never achieved without it and the money wasn't really an issue. I had plenty. "Yeah."

He chuckled. "Here, you'll always be a golden boy who made it. It's not the Super Bowl, but it's something. Right?" He was throwing me a bone, one I should've been grateful for, but instead, the weight of failure crushed me.

But what other options did I have?

"I'll probably be released this week, so when do you want me to start?" And I had another thought. "Can I pick my own staff?"

It had been a while since I'd been on a field. The hit I took in the first game this year had taken me out. How he knew about it made a lot more sense when I looked behind his desk and saw a picture of him and Olivia on some beach with the sun shining behind them and their arms wrapped around each other.

Everybody had somebody to love except for me. Maybe staying here at Glouster, where Avery was a respected professor, could change that for me. This had always been our place.

One Decade Ago

It'd been two days since the text I couldn't stop thinking about. During those two longest days of my life, I went to class, went to practice, but I didn't see Avery once. Didn't even run into her in the one class we had together, the same one she cut on Monday and then again today and she wasn't answering my texts. Any other girl, I would've shown up at her place with flowers or a giant stuffed animal, but those things wouldn't work on Avery.

I needed something better, but I honestly had no idea how to deal with a woman who wasn't as into me as I was into her. It never happened that way and Avery was too smart and too unshakable to fall for shenanigans and those were just about all I had to work with.

It wasn't until I was zipped into my costume, sitting in front of her house that I reconsidered the wisdom of this move. I looked ridiculous, but before I could drive away, she opened the door to my car and slid in. To her credit, she didn't laugh at the leather pants and matching jacket, my slicked-back hair, or the sound the leather on leather combo made when I moved.

More than that, though, while she took in my outfit, I almost fell out of the car when I looked at her. Apparently, we'd both decided on a wardrobe change. Dress to impress and all that, because she'd forsaken the thick eyeliner for a lighter line, the black lipstick for a shade closer to flamingo pink, her band t-shirt, also always in black, for a light pink cardigan and a button-down shirt. She'd also replaced her combat boots for a pair of low heels that matched the cardigan and lipstick.

One Bet

A laugh bubbled from her lips. "Would you look at us? We're the scary version of Danny and Sandy from Grease."

I smiled at the movie reference. At least she'd picked one where the guy got the girl. It gave me enough hope to want to twist toward her and kiss her, but this was Finn's jacket, and since he wasn't as big as me on top, it was too snug for so much movement. "I think we, well, mostly you, look amazing."

Her skin flushed and she looked down.

"Do you want to come in?" Hell, yes, I did, but I wasn't so sure I'd be able to get out of this car. She looked down at her hands when I didn't answer. "I was going to come to see you, but I couldn't figure out how to ride my bike in these shoes." She slipped the white shoe off and held it up to glare at it.

I really wanted to touch her. Kiss her. "I would've come to you."

Her smile was delicate as if another word

could shatter it and she'd dissolve. "This sweater's so itchy."

I nodded. "My jacket's too tight."

She wrapped her hand around the back of my neck and leaned in so I could feel her breath on my mouth. "I could lend you a shirt."

I lifted my arm and ignored the sound of the leather creaking, it didn't matter, all I cared about was Avery, this moment, and kissing her before she changed her mind and ignored me for another couple of days. "And I could help you with your swea…"

She kissed me, hard and needy, desperate, and with one hand moving between my seat and the door to slide me back. And if I'd thought I knew anything about heaven or pleasure before, I was wrong. I knew shit about it until she twisted to slide over the console onto my lap between my chest and the steering wheel.

Because I didn't want to scare her, didn't want to send her running out of the car with wrong ideas, or maybe the right ones, spinning through her head, I didn't run my fingers over the miles of bare leg lying across the console, or into the gap where she'd missed a button on her shirt. But it took every ounce of willpower I had to keep my hand in PG-13 land.

And I would've, but she twisted to unzip my jacket, her tongue still swirling inside my mouth. Her hand brushed against my skin, and I could've died from the sheer pleasure of it, but then she moved her lips down to my throat.

"You're supposed to wear a shirt with this jacket." Every word was punctuated by a kiss. Her mouth opened against my collarbone, and my dick twitched. I'd never wanted someone so badly. "I'm glad you didn't."

I wanted to touch her, to explore her with my hands and mouth, to taste her skin one delectable inch at a time, and just as I unfastened the second button of her shirt, a hard knock on the window made her jump and squeak out an almost quiet scream. She looked up and behind her. "Oh, shit."

She scrambled back to her side of the car, buttoning and panting, as I rolled down the window, chest still bare, hard on still at full attention.

We'd just been interrupted by the school chaplain, Avery's landlord.

Chapter 13

Avery

The diner was one of those mom-and-pop cafes with a black and white checkerboard floor, red leather booths and stools, and white Formica with gold glitter tabletops. A counter ran in front of a kitchen window, and the waitresses all wore pink dresses and little headpieces like old-time nurses used to wear. I'd worked here during my last two semesters at Glouster after Chaplain Dunn kicked me out of his garage apartment.

The sound of the waitresses shouting their orders through the window and pouring coffee from steaming pots without any additions of foam or whip and the clink of silverware made me feel young again. Younger when Keaton, who could've still passed for a guy in his twenties, came back from the bathroom and slid into the booth.

He smiled. "I should've known you'd pick here."

"I like the atmosphere." Homey, nostalgic, with Keaton. Which shouldn't have mattered since he was leaving in a few days and heading back to his life of football and supermodels.

"I like that hallway." He pointed to the corridor that led to the bathrooms on one side and the kitchen on the other. "I kissed a really pretty blonde waitress in that hallway."

He twisted. "And that back booth," he turned toward me again, "and on that counter."

Even ten years later, I still heated up with the onslaught of memories. "It wasn't *on* the counter, it was *at* the counter." And it was a memory best left ignored, but holy shit, it was a good memory. So good I had to shift to relieve the pressure low in my belly.

"In my dreams that night, it was *on* the counter." He grinned.

"You think they'll let us do a..." He shook his head and shrugged. "A re-enactment for old time's sake?"

Those were some good old times even if it had only been three days. "I'm a teacher now, I should probably keep my re-enactment in my pants." Though I could admit I still had some residual fantasies that involved this diner and Keaton.

"Damn, I knew I should've gone for it back then." His voice dropped low, sultry, so tempting. "Could've ticked that box off the bucket list."

"You need a better bucket list."

He laughed but reached across the table to

take my hand from my menu and hold it in his. "I missed you, Avery."

I didn't point out that I wasn't the one who moved or that hadn't changed my number in all these years, or that he'd been the one who started the beginning of our end. I smiled instead. "I missed you, too."

He gave my fingers a squeeze then let go. "No, you didn't. But that's okay. We didn't end things so well." I shook my head because I didn't know what to say. "But we're both here now and what happened was a long time ago." His thumb stroked my palm and the touch sent a thousand familiar, but exciting, sensations straight to my core. "We could start over."

My body screamed yes at the top of my lungs, but my brain shut that shit down. I couldn't set myself up for the Keaton roller coaster ride. Besides, he was leaving again. "Let's just enjoy this week the way we did before. Without the bad ending this time."

He tilted his head.

One Bet

"Okay." He nodded and picked up his glass of iced tea. "To this week and whatever comes after."

I chuckled. "You're so pushy."

And because I knew it, I could protect myself against his promises of after. But for now, I wanted to enjoy this week. To go back to that time when everything was good and fun. When I didn't know real heartbreak, and this time, I would protect myself. Not fall for him, but there was nothing wrong with simply enjoying time with another person.

So, I picked up my glass and clinked it with his. "To this week."

"Still so tough." He shook his head but smiled as he drank.

But he was wrong, I wasn't *still* so *tough*. Maybe I was still naïve or ignorant. But I wanted him and I was an adult now with no illusions about what would be or could be. This time, I was going in with my eyes wide open.

One Decade Ago

The boat was huge, opulent, fancier than anywhere I'd ever laid my damned head. The crystal chandelier probably cost more than a semester's tuition and it was on a boat for crying out loud. I sure as hell didn't belong here. "I can't stay here, Keaton."

"Just until you find somewhere to live, okay?" He ran his hands from my shoulders to my wrists then brought my knuckles to his mouth and kissed them softly, his gaze never leaving mine.

"What's your family going to say?" What would my family say? My mom would probably fall right in love with this place, but it was wrong. I needed to go back to Chaplain Dunn and beg his forgiveness for my behavior on the street in front of his house. Maybe if I waited until morning, that little vein in his temple would

One Bet

stop throbbing.

"My dad probably doesn't even remember he bought this boat." He chuckled and let go of my hands to turn and open the refrigerator. "Look, there's even food."

I didn't care about deli-sliced ham or bottles of imported beer. My rose-colored glasses slipped down my nose and realization of where I was standing came into sharp focus. I'd heard the rumors, on campus, they called this yacht *The Love Boat* because it was where all the Alphas brought their women. It was probably the boat Susie had ridden on with the Alpha who'd humiliated her. Oh, shit. It was Keaton, I should've known. Nothing that felt this good could be right, it just wasn't how my life worked.

I couldn't even look at him, the need for revenge burned through me. Not for myself, but for Susie. I pulled out my phone and dialed. As soon as he answered, I walked back out onto the deck leaving Keaton to his galley of food and tawdry props, wherever he had those hidden. "Alex, can I stay at your place tonight? And for a while?"

"Yeah. Why? What happened?"

Oh, the shame of my story, I wasn't quite ready for the show and tell. "Can we talk about it later? It's a shitty story and kind of embarrassing. I want to figure out how to sugar coat it before it gets to you."

He chuckled. "You bet. I'll leave the door unlocked."

Alex lived in an off-campus apartment so far away from the Alpha house I'd never have to see it or Keaton again and first thing tomorrow, I would drop my film class. Then, find ways to get to and from all my other classes without any chance of running into him.

Now that I had a plan for tomorrow, I only needed to figure out how to get to Alex's apartment. Taking an Uber or Lyft from the marina to the other side of town would eat up the last of this month's allowance, but no way was I getting back into a car with Keaton Shaw, a user of women and liar to the nth power. I used the app and then the stairs to get the hell off this boat and onto the dock. He could just keep the damned clothes he'd already carried inside. Alex would let me borrow something to wear.

He caught me at the edge of the dock. "Did I forget something in the car?"

In my own clothes, not this Barbie doll-reject costume, I would've been able to tell him to kiss my shiny ass, but I'd stopped being myself right around the time I had this stupid idea about Ryder and enlisted Keaton to help me. For a second, I missed the innocence of my own stupidity.

"No."

He chuckled. "Then what are you doing? Come back to the boat. I made you a sandwich."

"I didn't ask for a sandwich." I bit the words out, each syllable laced by fury and venom…

maybe with a smidge of hurt.

"I know. But...it's been a long night. I thought you might..."

"Well, you shouldn't think. It doesn't go well for you." Okay, now I was getting there. "You brought me back to your little love boat *thinking* I'd be so grateful we'd just get down and fuck, right? Then you could throw me away like you did, Susie."

"What? What the hell are you talking about? I didn't throw anyone away." He reached for me, but I jerked my arm to my side.

He could play dumb if he wanted to, but I knew what happened, the videos, the threats, and what I didn't know, I wasn't afraid to make up for effect. "She's the girl in the video. The one you whirled around the ocean in your fucking boat before you took her back to the frat house, screwed her, *then* humiliated her by having your friend throw her a 20 dollar bill." And right then I would've not been too proud to take his money to get the hell away from him.

One Bet

He huffed out a breath and turned, running his fingers through his hair before he spun to face me. "Couple things before you go. First, I didn't, and sure as shit didn't have someone, throw money at anyone. And second, I don't know shit about any video."

And I couldn't tell if he was lying or not. "Third, I can't drive this boat around the ocean, look at it."

He jabbed his finger toward the boat. "It's too fucking big for one person to captain. A *crew* brought it here."

Okay, it was big, but why have a boat just sitting in a marina that couldn't be driven. It didn't make sense and that made him a liar. Again. "I don't know how you did it or the logistics of moving a boat that big, but I know my friend got hurt…by you and your friends."

"I didn't hurt anyone." He shook his head. "Have I ever treated you like I don't worship the ground you walk on?"

"That's your act, it's why all the girls love

Keaton Shaw." A campus truth.

"Yes, and you can ask anyone I've ever dated. I would never do something like that." But something flickered in his eyes.

And it dispelled whatever little bit of logic had been trying to make its way through to the front of my brain. So, logic be damned, I went with emotion and revulsion and anger that was quickly turning to sadness. "Except to Susie."

"Who the fuck is Susie?"

"A little redhead you brought back to the Alpha house, banged brainless on camera, then sent out to be laughed at by all your Alpha asshole friends." I couldn't grasp the depths of her humiliation while I was almost drowning in my own. How could I have been so blind? So stupidly trusting? "I never want to see you again."

He threw his hands up and walked four steps then came back as my ride pulled up. "Avery, wait. Please don't go." He held out his hand even after I crossed my arms. "Please. I can't stand that you think this about me. It's killing me that you think I would be the guy who behaved that way."

"I don't know you well enough to know whether you would or not." I knew how he tasted. How his body felt under my hands. How he made my blood burn and my panties almost dissolve. But I didn't even know his middle name, or where he lived before college, if he had brothers and sisters, or if the way he treated me was an act and he truly was a womanizing asshat.

"Then stay. Get to know me, we can talk all night, I'll tell you anything you want to know." He moved closer, still holding out his hand. "Please. I like you so much I'm begging you to stay. Doesn't that mean anything?"

It did, even with all my circumstantial evidence against him. But I didn't want to be just another girl on the Alpha wall of conquests.

"All I'm asking for is the chance to explain.

To make you see I'm not a guy who would do that."

Although I would've bet any money I had in the world, that he knew who would. I also had a new mission in life, a reason other than a stupid case of lust for staying with Keaton that night, I slid my hand over his. "Okay."

Chapter 14

Keaton

I'd been in her house before, slept in her bed even, but I hadn't been sober enough to look around. She had turned this generic cottage into something homey and comfortable. Painted gray walls, red throw pillows that matched the red kitchen accents and the runner on the dining table. Splashes of red in the paintings, and framed pictures on a mantle sans fireplace hanging on the single white wall.

"This is nice, Avery." She handed me a

bottle of beer and took a long drink from her own. I liked that she was nervous because I was too. It had been a long time since I'd held her, and I wanted to do it again.

"You want the tour?" Her cheeks reddened as she held out her free hand.

Something told me she didn't mean a walk-through of her house.

"Yeah." I stood and she used her beer bottle to point. "Kitchen. Dining room. Living room. Bathroom." She'd spun in almost a circle before she pulled me behind her to a closed door. "Bedroom."

I smiled because it would've been impossible not to. "I've been in here before."

"Not sober." She took our bottles and set them on a dresser almost as tall as she was. Then she lifted my hand again and pulled me toward the bed. "It's a completely different experience when you're sober."

She kissed my throat near my collarbone

then moved her way up to nibble gently on my earlobe.

"What are you doing?" Not that I minded, I rather liked slipping my arms around her and pulling her hips into line with mine.

"Enjoying this week." To emphasize her point, she twisted the button on my shirt free and pressed a kiss against the skin she'd just exposed. As she made her way down to my stomach, my body came alive, and there was no reason to think anymore. I hadn't ever stopped wanting Avery, even after everything that happened. But neither did I want this to end too soon, so when she went after my belt and button fly, I pulled her up to kiss me.

My chest was bare, and I wanted more skin-to-skin contact. "Fair is fair."

I pushed the sweater she'd worn over her tank top from her shoulders so it landed on the floor behind her, and with my index finger, I lowered one strap to her biceps so I could taste her shoulder. Oh God, she was as perfect as I remembered.

She moaned as I moved from her shoulder across her collarbone to the other side. The sound went straight to my dick and while I wanted this to last longer than the three minutes I doubted it would, I also wanted her now. Right now.

But if this was the one time we would be together, and while I was hopeful that it would turn into something more, I couldn't say for sure, I wanted it to be something she'd remember. For all my thoughts of slowing this down, Avery flung her top behind her, then unfastened her bra before she undid the skirt, so it pooled at her feet. She stood naked in front of me and I couldn't stop staring, she was perfect. From the curve of her neck to the one at her hip.

"You haven't had underwear on all night under that skirt?" A detail I would've definitely taken advantage of had I known.

One Bet

"Not since I decided I wanted to bring you back here." This time I didn't stop her, couldn't have, wouldn't have, as she unfastened my pants and shoved them, along with my boxers, to my ankles.

"If you would've told me, the ride home would've been way more interesting."

She wrapped her hand around me and stroked, long, slow, and firm. Perfect. Then she gave me a dirty grin before she spoke. "It was interesting, anyway. If you knew the thoughts in my head while I watched your fingers wrapped around the steering wheel."

She rubbed her breasts against my chest as she continued caressing my cock. "When you licked your lips, I wanted to lay the seat back and slide my skirt up to touch myself."

Oh God, she'd done that for me once, and I had savored that memory on many a lonely night. But now, I wanted to be the one who touched her, who felt her wetness on my fingers…on my tongue…on my dick.

I let my hand fall over the arch at her hip and around to glide against her clit. She gasped but tilted her head and closed her eyes as I let it swipe a second time before I cupped her mound and used my thumb to tease her as I slipped a finger inside. Oh. Still so tight, so wet.

"Avery." I couldn't manage more than her name. "Lie down."

I liked that I didn't have to tell her twice. I also liked looking at her as she did what I told her to do, she was a pure seductress. I kicked off my jeans and reclined next to her, lifted on my elbow so I could let my gaze follow my finger down her chest to circle her nipple, then across to the other as I licked a circle around the first. It pebbled and I blew softly so she pulled in a deep breath and held it when I sucked lightly. Her body was so responsive, and I wanted to see it all, feel it close around me.

One Bet

She held my head to her breast for a minute until I pulled away and moved my fingers over the slight curve of her belly, over a scar just below her last rib. I'd ask how she got it later. Now, I wanted to hear her whimper, cry out my name. When I moved down with my hand, slid my hand between her legs, working my finger in and out, then shifted to lie between her knees, she arched her back and moaned.

She tasted sweet and salty, and if I lived to be a hundred years old, I would always love doing this with her. Especially when her muscles tightened, and I could lap up the sweetness of her orgasm and know I helped her get there. She cried out, dug her fingernails into my shoulders, and pulled me up to hang over her.

"Please tell me you have a condom."

I did, not because I planned anything involving us, but because putting a condom in my wallet was as natural as sticking my money in there. "Hang on." I reached for my pants and yanked out the foil packet. She took it from me, pushed me onto my back, and tore it open with her teeth then rolled it down my cock with such deft fingers that I almost came before she finished.

I almost didn't last long enough for her to climb on top of me and lower herself onto my pulsing dick. Oh fuck. Oh fuck. Oh *fuck*. She was amazing. And every move of her hips, every circular motion brought me closer to the edge of passion and reason and sanity. Avery Stroh was a goddess. Always had been, and now she was riding me with her back arched and her hips thrusting, circling, bouncing until I was sure I wouldn't survive the pleasure.

My body tensed as she leaned over and kissed me hard and desperate, her moans vibrating with mine as we came apart together. I could only gasp as the world went out of focus and then, slowly, reality came back to me.

"It's been too long since we did that." She collapsed against my chest, with my dick still inside her. The change in position, the way her muscles contracted against me, made me want her again.

I smiled. "Well, maybe we should make up for the lost time."

It was a wish more than a suggestion, but she lifted her head and grinned. "Can you?"

I flipped us so she was beneath me. "I guess we'll see."

The girl I'd known back then had grown into the woman beneath me and I wouldn't be able to let her go this time. Not like I had back then. I just had to figure out if she felt the same way.

One Decade Ago

I couldn't stand the look on her face, the distrust I could see in those stormy gray eyes. She wouldn't sit beside me, wouldn't even look at me, but she was here, so I had a chance. And I didn't want to ruin it by pushing her or saying the wrong thing. But the silence was killing me.

"Avery."

She lifted her head as if seeing me, but she focused on something over my shoulder and it was killing me.

"What's your middle name? Where do you live? Why me?" She looked down at the sweater she'd pulled back around her then reached to slide off one of her shoes and hold it up. "I could understand if this was the shoe I wore all the time, but it isn't and it probably never will be, so that begs the question, again, why me?"

I hadn't thought about it much myself outside of the fact I liked her. She wasn't the same carbon copy I'd dated for the last four years and then there was the bet. Which didn't really matter but was still there in the background where I hoped it would stay until I could talk to Ryder and get out of it.

So, I started with the easy questions. "My middle name is Matthew, I grew up in Texas just a little west of Dallas and I like who you are. I like who I am when we're in a room together." Now she looked at me and I wanted to be honest. "I haven't always been the most stand-up guy when it comes to dating."

She frowned.

"But I've never videoed myself with a girl, ever. Sex is private, and I don't take it lightly. I wouldn't do that to your friend."

"But you've hurt other girls?"

I nodded. "But not because I lied to them or humiliated them. Sometimes, when things don't work out, they just don't and when it isn't the same for both people, one gets hurt."

She rolled her eyes. "That sounds like a line every guy uses."

"Sometimes we all say the same thing

because it's true. You've been in relationships, did you always walk away with a broken heart or did you give a couple?"

And before I even finished, I knew I was an idiot. Her eyes narrowed and her mouth tightened. "No. I haven't. Either way. Guys don't look at girls like me."

What? Even with her torn leggings and enough eyeliner for every girl on campus, she was beautiful, and I couldn't imagine a world where men didn't look at her. "Why would you think that?"

I wanted to move beside her, touch the curve of her face, and look into her eyes so she could see how much I liked her. But I didn't because I couldn't stand the thought of her pushing me away. "Did you know that at any given time, I have six or eight pens in my backpack? I never needed your pen, I just wanted to talk to you."

"So, you started off by lying to me?" Her dark eyebrow quirked over her left eye and it did something to me I wasn't expecting, something that made me stare at her even longer. I was, to put it plainly, afraid that if I lied she'd have my balls in a vice in an instant.

"Wow." If she wasn't taking pre-law classes, the legal world was being cheated of a great mind. "Okay, yeah. I did, but if I would have walked up to you and just started a conversation with you, what would you have done?"

Now she looked at her hands, and we both knew the answer to that.

"And I would never lie to you now, I wish you could believe that." I knew why she couldn't. I'd given her no reason to do anything but doubt my word, I just didn't want to get hung up on it. Not with her, but I could admit it. "You know, I'm scared too, Avery. I haven't felt this way about anyone before. Not this fast, not ever and I don't want to get hurt either, but I'm here with you right now because you're worth the risk and because I don't want to look for excuses to not be with you."

Oh no. Her eyes flashed and that was the part she latched onto.

"I'm not looking for excuses."

Because there was nothing I could say to change her mind, I pointed my gaze at hers and spoke soft, but firm. "Bullshit."

She cocked one eyebrow and tilted her head. "Excuse me?"

And if I was going to blow it, I would blow it big because Keaton Shaw never did anything halfway. No matter how much it broke my heart.

"What happened to your friend didn't happen to you and I get it. You're mad on her behalf, but to use it as an *excuse* to stop seeing me is bullshit." I wiped my palms together. Never had they been so sweaty, or had I been so nervous over a woman's reaction. "I'll go if you want, or take you to your friend's house, and we don't ever have to talk again, but I didn't hurt your friend. I hope you know that."

I waited a second. "All you have to do is tell me to go."

She closed her eyes, and I held my breath until she said, "I don't want to."

And no words in my life had ever made me happier.

Chapter 15

Avery

I left the self-recriminations outside of the bedroom, but oh boy were they waiting for me when I dragged myself to the kitchen for coffee. He was leaving in days, not weeks or months, days.

Days.

Days.

But right now, he was in my room, in my bed, under my blankets.

Correction, he was walking through my

living room, shirtless, adorably disheveled, smiling, and coming right at me.

The morning after nerves, an absence of coherent thought, and a numb tongue came together all at once. Yep. I had about two seconds to get my shit together before he…oh yeah…hugged me. "Good morning."

How did he still manage to smell so good? And look so good? And feel…so good? "Good morning."

He kissed the top of my head then laid his cheek over the spot. "You have plans Friday night?"

I never had plans. The question was, did I want him to know that.

"No." If I was only going to have a few more days with him, I wanted every minute I could get. Selfish and stupid as it was.

"Do you remember Jameson King?"

Of course, I did, he was part of the scandal that rocked Glouster. But I hadn't really known him. "Not really."

"We played football together. He got hurt senior year." When I shook my head because the memory of that time still caused me to lose my breath and my head to hurt, he let me go. "He asked me to have dinner with him and his wife Friday."

He chewed his lip as the coffee maker finished its final dribble into the pot and I poured two steaming mugs of Colombian brew. "Said I could bring a date."

That sounded a little too much like relationship stuff that would leave me with a broken heart when he left. "I don't know, Keaton, that's your friend. I don't want to get in the way of all the reminiscing about your glory days."

Mostly I didn't want to sit in a room with someone who had a part in making me a college cliché.

"All right." He cocked his head. "Even if my friend, Jameson, is married to your friend, Susie?"

Susie? The love of Alex's life? The reason he was walking around with a three-karat diamond in his pocket? It had to be a mistake. "What, now?"

"Three kids, her red hair, his curls. Your fake boyfriend kissed her a thousand times the other night." He stared at me, but I couldn't process.

I could only see Alex holding that ring box, smiling with just the slightest glow of pink staining his cheeks, and she was married.

"Anyway. If you don't want to go, I guess I'll find out what's going on myself." He laid his hand over mine. "I have some other news too."

I wasn't really interested in his news right then. I shoved my hands through my hair, thoughts flitting around like startled caged birds. I needed to call Alex, warn him. When that was done I wanted to kill Susie. How could she lie to Alex? He wasn't disposable. Anger on my best friend's behalf burned in my gut.

"Did you know?" It might've sounded more like an accusation than I meant it to.

"No. Jameson was my driver yesterday and it came up."

"Alex came up?" I didn't know or remember Jameson, but I knew Alex, and he would be heartbroken, devastated and I didn't want to be the one to tell him, but I also didn't want to know and not tell him.

"No."

Normally, in a situation like this, I would call Alex. He always knew what to do.

"Do I tell him?" I didn't wait for an answer. "I have to tell him. If he finds out that I knew…"

It would kill him. A new thought occurred to me and I looked up at Keaton with a hint of fear in my eyes. "Are you going to tell Jameson?"

Oh shit. What if Jameson killed Alex? I couldn't wrap my head around one thought long enough to decide anything.

Keaton took my mug from my hand and put it on the counter so he could brace a hand on each of my shoulders. "Avery, we don't know anything. Maybe…there's an explanation."

"For cheating? For leading Alex on then going home to her husband and kids?" This was the same kind of injustice she'd spray-painted the Alpha house for. Not exactly the same, but a lie was a lie. "Do you have any idea how many times we graffitied the Alpha house because of what happened to her, for the way she was treated? Because she got treated like she didn't matter."

Not to mention my article which was best left in the past, way in the past.

"And now, she's doing the same thing, well, kind of, to Alex and to Jameson." That bitch. A little bit of the old, kick-ass first, ask questions later me poked her head out from wherever she'd been hiding all these years.

"We don't know everything."

"What's there to know? She has a husband and kids, and she was out with us the other night porn-kissing my best friend in a bar. What detail do I still need to know, Keaton?" And if he thought any of this was okay, we had nothing left to say to each other.

"I don't know, but…maybe we should wait and talk to her first."

Keaton was the kind of guy who gave the benefit of the doubt. Maybe because of the way he grew up or maybe because he was just good-hearted. But I wasn't so easy to get along with. I saw things for what they were and the old me spoke up about it. Unless someone I cared about asked me not to.

One Decade Ago

I should've known when I'd smashed my cell phone screen into a spider web of broken glass on the edge of the bathtub, and when I missed the bus from the marina to Glouster, and when I received my first C on a test, in my life, that I should've gone home and crawled back in bed. My nice warm boat bed with the thousand count sheets and the man who'd talked to me until the wee hours then held me until his alarm blared for his five-a.m. practice.

I never should've left the boat. At least then I wouldn't have been so surprised to return to the boat and find the older version of Keaton holding a pair of my fishnet stockings by the toe and staring at me like he'd just found the holy grail.

I wanted to run, and I didn't know why, instead, I stood watching him, thinking nothing more than he was what Keaton would look like in twenty years. I breathed out, and he turned to look me up and down. "Yours, I presume?"

Not an impressively brilliant deduction since I was wearing the matching pair and he'd spent a few seconds gawking at them, I nodded.

He chuckled and held out the stocking to me. I snatched it and hid it behind my back. "I have to say, you're not the usual kind of girl Keaton brings to the boat."

Yeah. No shit. My skin had to be fifty or

sixty shades of red since my cheeks were on fire. But it wasn't every day I trespassed on a boat to find a man holding my intimate garments pinched between his fingers. "Well, he's expanding his horizons."

Oh no, this wasn't going well.

"I see that." Oh hell, they had the same grin. "Do you happen to know where Keaton is?"

And as if he'd been summoned by his dad's question, Keaton slid open the door and stepped through. "Dad!"

And they hugged with what sounded like some painful back slapping and a round of laughter.

"I was just getting to know your…friend." I could've done without the grimace attached to the last word, but I kept my fake, pasty smile in place.

Keaton ignored it and stepped back to stand about halfway between me and his dad. "I didn't know you were coming this week."

"Yes, well, we need to talk. Maybe

your *friend* could give us a minute?" He looked at me, smiled again, and lifted his eyebrows.

It was a hint to get out. "I'll just…" I pointed behind me to the door. "Right."

Leaving made sense. I walked out onto the deck and left using the small ramp that led from the boat to the dock. I'd almost made it to the bus stop when Keaton caught me by the arm.

"Where are you going?"

"Somewhere away, where I can forget the fact that I walked onto your *dad's* boat to find him holding up my…" I handed him the stocking and turned to continue walking. "Away."

Keaton moved to block my path and I swerved around him. "Avery, wait. My dad wants to go to dinner. Please."

"Are you out of your mind? I'm not going to dinner with you. I'm not the kind of girl you usually date or bring to dinner." His dad's words had affected me, and they hurt even though they were his and not Keaton's. "Or to your boat."

I plopped down on the bench inside the bus shelter hard enough that the whole structure rattled, and I hurt my tailbone.

He sat beside me. "If you want to get to know me, really know me, this is how you do it."

I shot him a glare I only half felt. "It isn't fair to use my own shit against me."

But I took his hand when he stood and offered it, then walked beside him back to the boat. An hour later, we were sitting at a table in a restaurant with a dress code I violated in about ten ways.

Of all the places I'd ever been and people I'd ever met, I'd never felt so out of my element. Everyone in the restaurant, including Keaton and his dad, was perfectly coiffed in designer makeup and clothes. I had my thrift store cardigan, scuffed heels, and mostly fresh face and it only took about forty seconds after we sat for me to knock my water glass into the candle on the table which fell over. Thankfully, the water doused the flame before I could catch the whole place on fire, but the water was heading right for Mr. Shaw and me, quick thinking, stood and threw my napkin at the moving puddle, but I wasn't the quarterback at the table so, of course, the napkin landed on Keaton's dad's head and the water dripped off the table onto his lap.

"I'm so sorry. I'm not clumsy. I'm just nervous." I was babbling, standing and babbling as Keaton's dad pulled my napkin from his hair, which still looked remarkably good. "Do you use hairspray? Because, wow."

Next to me, Keaton chuckled, and I sank back to my chair, wishing I could shrivel and die, then his dad smiled. "I use gel."

Of the three people at our table, I was the only one who didn't find this funny. I sighed and smoothed my sweaty hands down the front of my skirt, wishing I still had a veil of hair to hide behind. Keaton squeezed my hand under the table as his dad watched us. "So, Ashley, Keaton tells me you've been helping him with his classes."

Did I look like an Ashley? "It's Avery. And we study together, but…"

We hadn't studied much, and he didn't really seem to need my help.

"Yes, well, Keaton's always been a better athlete than he has been a student." His tone went dry and the insult wasn't just implied.

Now it was my turn to squeeze his hand. "Well, the school has certainly benefited from his athletic ability. Three championships in three years."

"Football isn't a career, Avery." As he spoke to me, he glanced at Keaton. "For his brother maybe, but Keaton doesn't have that kind of talent."

Thanks to our midnight chat, I already knew his brother had been killed in Afghanistan. Keaton fiddled with one of his three forks, tapping his finger on the edge. "I think Keaton's talent speaks for itself."

"Avery, don't." I glanced at him, saw the embarrassment, and my heart ached for him. My mom might not have been rich or even had enough money to afford school lunches when I was a kid, but she loved me, and she was proud of everything I had ever accomplished or even attempted. As I was about to inform Mr. Shaw of the error of his parenting ways, Keaton looked up at me and smiled, then turned to his father.

"Julian was a great ballplayer, Dad." His voice was soft, almost soothing.

I sat back, my understanding of Keaton a little greater, my blossoming feelings a little deeper. He might have had more stuff, but I had the better life.

Chapter 16

Keaton

I'd forgotten how much I loved being on the practice field at Glouster. Here, I was a god. Celebrated. Revered. Talented. What I wasn't, was a has-been, not injured or damaged and it felt really good.

It also kept my mind off Avery. Well, mostly, until I looked up at the storm clouds and thought of her eyes. It took me a few minutes to refocus and that was how my afternoon worked. Instead of watching practice, planning how I would help, a hundred things made me think of Avery. And smile. And hope. Until finally I left the stadium. I wanted to find her, just see her. Instead, I walked out of the player entrance to the stadium and stopped.

I didn't think this moment would come. But there he was. Ryder Kennedy, older, fatter, and a lot angrier.

"The great Keaton Shaw." He pushed off the wall and straightened. "Mr. Big Time."

I stared at him, it had been years and still, he looked the same. Same blonde hair, same green eyes. He'd put on some weight, but that came when the working out stopped and the muscle we'd worked so hard to build turned to fat before we could prevent it. But he wasn't supposed to be here. I hadn't been invited back to the fraternity house or the college for this hundred-year celebration of the Alphas. And his appearance made red flags billow through my mind.

"Ryder."

I walked past and he fell into step beside me.

"What? You can't stop and chat with an old friend?" He scoffed. "Figures."

He'd been a friend once, my best friend. But he hadn't just hurt Avery. And after everything he'd done, I couldn't just forgive and forget. He grabbed my shoulder and yanked so that I twisted toward him. Fucker. I gave him a shove. Softer than I would have if we didn't have history. Softer than he deserved, but he fell into the wall anyway.

He chuckled and held up both hands as if surrendering. "Oh, come on, Keats. I just wanted to say hey to an old friend. No harm. No foul. Right?"

I didn't answer because, with Ryder, the one I'd known then anyway, there was always a layer of harm and foul to everything he touched. "How's your girl? Heard she's a teacher now."

My internal asshole-radar beeped, his tone,

the implied threat, meant something. He had a plan. It was why he'd made an appearance here, in a place where he wasn't welcome. Only he'd showed his hand now. Part of it at least, and I only had to figure out what cards he still had up his sleeve.

Friends close. Enemies closer

"She's great." And she was gonna kill me. "Why don't you come out for drinks with us one of these nights? We can catch up."

He had that same evil gleam in his eyes a decade later.

"Yeah. I think I'd like that." My stomach churned when he repeated the sentiment, this time smug enough I almost reconsidered, almost. "I think I would definitely like that."

But he'd gotten one over on me before because I didn't know exactly the kinds of things he was capable of, now I knew and no way would he win again.

One Decade Ago

Practice sucked, Ryder hadn't even shown. Avery wasn't answering her phone, and I just wanted to see her. Not a minute of the day went by without me calculating how long before I would be with her again.

I left the stadium, drove straight to the marina, and climbed out of my car just as Ryder walked up the dock. He gave me a wave. "Hey, buddy."

I waited until he was almost standing in front of me. "Where were you?"

"Out on the water." He grinned. "Had a date."

But he hadn't come from the direction of his boat. I frowned and looked down the marina to the slip where his dad kept the family yacht. He chuckled. "Then I stopped by yours to see if you made it out of practice yet." He clapped a hand on my shoulder and laughed. "God, you're so suspicious."

One Bet

I laughed too, he was my best friend. Whatever his excuse, he wouldn't do anything to hurt me, and he'd been on the boat without me about a thousand times. "Yeah."

Now was my chance to use our friendship in a way I never had before. "I'm glad you're here. I've been wanting to talk to you about something."

"Yeah? What's that?" He turned to walk beside me back to the boat.

I waited until we were both on the deck, beers in hand, loungers reclined. "You know that…bet we made?" I wanted out. I liked Avery the way she was and there was no way she still wanted Ryder, so…no harm, no foul as long as I ended it before she found out.

He tipped back his beer and nodded then wiped his mouth with the back of his hand. Something was off and he was angry now.

"What about it?" He nodded, but the rage didn't leave his eyes. "Oh, you heard about Finn and Jameson taking some of my action on our bet? Don't worry. A lot of the other guys bet on you."

"You told other people about it?" Oh God, too many people knowing or being in on it...I had to tell Avery before someone else did. "I need to call the whole thing off. It's just I really like Avery and I don't want...this...to come between us."

"You want out of the bet?" I nodded and he glared, his mouth dropping open enough for a scoff to escape. "For her?"

"I think I could have something real with her."

He chuckled and shook his head.

"Real. With her. That's funny." When I didn't join in laughing, he sobered. "Oh, you're serious. Wow. I'm sorry, Keats. It's just she isn't our...kind of girl."

Sometimes his arrogance amazed even me, and I knew him better than I knew anyone else. "What's our kind of girl, Ryder?"

"The kind we bet you could make her into.

A Sigma. A Kappa. But hey, it's good. You want to dabble in the dark arts, good on you. More Kappas and Sigmas for me." He shrugged again. "But, no can do on the bet. I used the money to finance the party Friday. Whole school's betting on this thing." He shrugged as if he was powerless in the whole matter.

How had he managed to spread the word so far in less than a week without either Avery or me hearing about it? And how the hell could I make it all stop?

"Why would you do that?"

Ryder laughed. "Oh, come on. You can't be serious. You like her? Really?" And I didn't answer immediately. That was my fault, the first time I let her down. Thank God she wasn't there to know about it.

Chapter 17

Avery

I chose the pier where a traveling carnival would be leaving soon. This was the last place Alex and I had really been best friends before we gave into adulthood. Ten years ago. We'd drowned my embarrassment in cotton candy, dispelled my humiliation with funnel cake, and shot away my misery with little pellets aimed at metal ducks. Then he'd let me cry my eyes out on the Ferris wheel while he held me.

"Hey." He smiled and hugged me like we

hadn't just seen each other two days ago. "Are you okay?"

No, I wasn't okay. I didn't want to have to tell him what I had to tell him because I wanted to buy time and maybe even soak up the nostalgia, I slipped my arm through his. "Let's walk."

He grinned. "I know what you're doing, you're leading me to the cotton candy."

I wished a hankering for sugar was my only motive. It was chilly, fall had come to Maine and the place was almost abandoned. But the smell of the carnival, grease on the squeaking rides, food only available from carnies, childhood in one breath. It carried on the wind and made me smile. "How about the Ferris wheel?"

He shot me a side-eyed glance. "Alright." But as we waited in line, our dynamic changed. He wasn't waiting for me to break his heart. "I have to tell you something, Avery."

"Okay." And I let him go first because I

didn't want to. Because I didn't want to be the one who made the hurt appear in his eyes.

He paused for a long time while we waited for the ride to stop. "I love you."

We said it all the time before we hung up the phone, but curiously, we'd never said it in person. Probably because we didn't spend time together in person. But then I looked at him. He didn't love me the way I loved him. He was hearts and flowers, meet the parents and pick a hall kind of loving me. "What about Susie?"

My voice was a squeak. A half, no, third of its usual tone.

"She's just…a friend I thought I was falling in love with until I saw you." He sighed. "I know. Alright? I know. You and I are…we're us."

He shook his head. "I mean, what am I doing? Right? I love you and I'm sleeping with her."

I didn't answer because I didn't know what to say.

"And now you're back with Keaton…right?"

I didn't have an answer for that either. If sleeping together didn't mean Alex was with Susie, then how could it mean I was with Keaton?

"Of course, you are. Because he's him."

I couldn't form anything coherent in my mind to get out of my mouth.

"Alex…" He'd seemed so into Susie. "You bought her a ring."

"I didn't give it to her. Because I saw you and I couldn't. She's not the one. You are."

"Me?" But we hadn't done more than talk on the phone in a decade. Although we did talk at least once a week. Alex loved me. In the way, he wasn't supposed to love me.

And he deserved more than a lie. Deserved better than me. He deserved someone who loved him back, who wanted to take him to bed every night and wake up with him every morning and I didn't. Not him. But admitting my feelings for someone else just to prove my point seemed cruel, so, I didn't. But saying nothing seemed worse.

"Alex…" I probably should've had something in mind before I tried to speak. As it was, all I had was his name, said in a kind of helpless moan.

"Ever since that night when you showed up at my place and asked for my help when you kissed me…I love you, Avery, I always have. It's you. Always you."

There was no space in my head, no room for me to process any more information.

"I have to go, Alex." I turned to leave.

"Please, Avery…" He laid his hand on my shoulder and leaned in to kiss me. I waited for something…anything…a tingle, a vibration, a tremor. And I wanted there to be something because this was Alex, and a relationship with him would be easy and based on more than attraction, but I didn't feel so much as a waiver. He pulled back. "We make sense, Avery, together, you and I make sense. Who better to be with than my best friend? We already tell each other everything."

Clearly not everything. "If we don't work out, we lose everything."

He took my face between his hands. "But if we do work out, we have everything. You're already the person I can't wait to talk to. The one I tell all my stupid shit and I don't even mind when you tell me it's stupid shit."

I was paralyzed, but Alex kept going.

"I've waited all these years for the time to be right, for us to be in the same place at the same time. I waited for perfection, but seeing you, you are the perfection and nothing else matters."

I couldn't think of anything to say so I didn't try, but suddenly Susie being married to Jameson didn't seem like such a big deal.

"I'll tell Susie and you can tell Keaton and we can start our life together. You and me, here or in Chicago." Oh yeah. Alex lived halfway across the country now. It was why, for the last ten years, we'd only talked on the phone. And God, I wished we could go back to that right now, that I didn't have to look into his puppy dog brown eyes and see the hope shining there, didn't have to hear the soft gasp when he realized I didn't feel the same way.

Or watch him turn to walk away. How did I not know?

Maybe I did. Maybe I just didn't want to admit it because then losing my best friend was my own fault.

One Decade Ago

Alex followed me through the store, his face so red I was afraid he might explode as we walked among the racks of lingerie and half-dressed mannequins. I never shopped retail, so the price tags were quite the culture shock for me, but Alex wasn't buying and he wasn't wearing, so his red-faced discomfort didn't make much sense to me. We always shopped together.

"What about this one?" I held the bra and panty set up for him to give me his yea or nay. So far, we were fifteen nays deep, and I was no closer to finding that something special to wear for Keaton than I was to knowing what the hell was wrong with Alex. Times like this, I almost regretted not having friends who were girls.

Alex grumbled another no, and I stared at his glum face. "Just pick something and wear it, Avery. He isn't going to care."

Uh-oh. Something was wrong with Alex. In all the time we'd ever spent together, he was never short-tempered with me. "Are you okay?"

He sighed. "I just don't want to spend all afternoon in a lingerie shop with you preparing for your big night with Football Boy." He lowered his voice. "He isn't going to give a shit what you wear when he's just gonna…"

He shook his head and looked away from me.

And maybe he was right, but I wanted tonight to be perfect. I wanted our first time, my first time, to be amazing and wonderful. That meant undergarments that either matched my eyes, made my skin look deeper and darker, or accentuated the curve of my ass while simultaneously downplaying the cellulite dimples I wouldn't be able to hide while I was mostly naked, and I needed to do it on a budget.

I pawed through another rack while Alex leaned against the wall, arms crossed, scowl in place. "What is it about this guy anyway?"

"He's just…" What was it? "I like him."

"Doesn't mean you have to fuck him."

"Alex!" I spun in a tight circle to make sure no one had heard his crass characterization of my plans for the night before I glared at him. "What the hell is wrong with you?"

He sighed. "I just don't think he should be pressuring you to sleep with him. You hardly know him."

One Bet

Pressuring me? Quite the opposite. He'd slept with me three nights now and hadn't done more than hold me even though I'd seen and "accidentally" felt how hard he was. Tonight, I was going to surprise him with soft music and lingerie. A yes, he could see.

But right now, I had to figure out Alex and what to do to fix whatever was wrong with him. I hated that he was so upset. "We could see a movie if you want to. My treat." Between school, Keaton, and my new job at the diner, we hadn't had much time to spend together. And it had only been a week, but even with being so busy, it felt like a year.

He stared at me. "I gotta go."

But he didn't move, and I didn't want him to.

"Alex?"

Without another word, he turned and stalked out of the store. Instead of selecting anything special, I just made a random selection, and the salesgirl chuckled when I set two of the bra and panty sets on the counter. "Oh, girl. Good choice. Definitely make-up worthy."

Covergirl or a big old apology kind of make-up? But I didn't want to ask, so I just agreed. "Yeah."

"And don't worry, once he sees you in this thing, he's gonna forget whatever made him storm out of here." She kept the hangers and stuffed my purchases into a fur-lined, zebra stripe bag.

"Oh, he's not my...I bought these for someone else." But that didn't explain why I was telling my business to a complete stranger.

She chuckled. "Well, that poor guy has it bad for you."

Oh, what did she know? I took my bag, stuffed it into my purse, and walked back to the marina since Alex was my ride, and he'd left in a huff. But it was okay because I practically floated on a cloud thinking of Keaton and that we would finally be together tonight.

Chapter 18

Keaton

Something was off, different than this morning. Ordinarily, I didn't mind if she stared at me, but she'd been looking through me for more than an hour while she pretended to eat the Chinese take-out that had been waiting for me when I arrived.

I'd just stuffed a dumpling in my mouth when she sighed. "We aren't friends."

She spoke as if she'd just discovered electricity as if surprised by her statement.

"We're not?" I liked to think we were.

"We're people who know each other and sleep together." She shook her head and leaned back in her chair. "But we're not friends. I don't call you when I've had a bad day."

I smiled, but I had a bad feeling in my stomach, so I sat back and crossed my arms. "You could."

Seeing her name on my phone screen made me inordinately happy. "I'd like that."

"You don't even know about Billy Pruett."

If I was supposed to be following this conversation, she was going to be a bit let down. "Who's Billy Pruett?"

"It doesn't matter, you don't know him." She shook her head.

"I mean, I could tell you and you would be, I don't know, sympathetic or whatever, but I'd only be telling you because you don't know, not because you found me crying after he ran off and left me on the swings then told everybody I had bad breath." She sighed as if she'd just summed up everything in that one mixed-up explanation.

And I had no idea what I was supposed to say to that. But I felt her slipping away from me, pointing out my flaws and preparing to use them against me. "Avery, what's going on? Who's Billy Pruett, and why does he matter tonight?"

She chuckled. "He doesn't matter. He's the first boy I ever kissed. When I was eleven and the point isn't about Billy. It's that you don't know about him. We don't have a good foundation. I mean, I know about you because you tell me things, but I don't tell you stuff."

She stood and took my half-finished plate to scrape into the disposal in the sink before she spun to face me again, this time pointing a fork. "I don't tell you stuff."

"Why not?"

She tossed the fork into the sink, and I couldn't stand not touching her anymore because if this was going to be the last time, I was going to make it last. I stood, moved behind her to slide my arms around her waist and pull her back into my chest.

"Maybe I don't trust you." She spoke softly, and the syllables stuttered out as if she wasn't even sure she wanted to say the words.

When I used my chin to move her hair back, she tilted her head so I could reach the spot under her ear that she liked kissed.

"Why don't you trust me?" I continued to nuzzle her hair and tried not to move too much. She might scamper away.

It took her an extra second to answer, maybe because I slid my hand under the hem of her shirt and rubbed my thumb in a little circle around her belly button. "History, and because I don't know you very well."

I took her earlobe into my mouth and sucked so that her breath hitched.

"Oh, you know me," I answered. It probably wasn't what she was talking about, but I spun her around to face me. "You know I like being with you and touching you, holding you, and sleeping with you tucked in beside me."

She pulled away from me. Far enough that I couldn't use my lips, my breath, my hands to distract her.

"Avery, I love talking to you, hearing you go on about books you love and movies that make you cry or laugh. I love just being in the same room as you because you might smile, and if I'm in the same place, I get to see it. I might not know who Billy Pruett is, although I can say, he sounds like an asshole, but we don't have to know everything about each other right away for us to know how we feel about each other."

"It's not right away, we've known each other for years now and I know what I've read about you in the papers over the years and what you told me a long time ago. But that's it." She cleared her throat and took two beers out of the refrigerator. As she opened mine, I smiled even though I could feel the end coming. She handed me my beer then opened hers and took a long drink. A very long drink before she swiped her hand over her mouth and breathed out through her nose. "Alex is in love with me."

I sat down. "Now I know something." Alex? The same guy who was sleeping with Jameson's wife? The guy who'd been her friend in college? My stomach tightened. When did Alex Rhodes become the guy all the girls wanted? "Do you love him?"

"I should. I know everything about him." She sat down and folded her hands on the table. "He's a good person. My best friend."

"But do you love him?" I held my breath as I waited for her answer. This one could hurt.

She shook her head.

"No." She closed her eyes. "Not like he wants me to."

Now I sat across from her because when the answer to my next question came, I would probably need to be sitting. "Do you need time to figure out…what you want?"

She took a minute longer than was good for

my ego then blew out another slow breath and stood to hold out her hand to me. "I think so. Thank you."

My heart thudded to a stop, and I breathed out slowly against the pain in my gut. "Okay. I'll just uh…"

I nodded to the door. "And you can…"

My throat was thick, and I couldn't finish. Instead, I grabbed my jacket and headed for the door.

She let me go to the door and open it, walk out and onto the porch then down the steps to come around the driver's side of my car when she rushed outside.

"Keaton, wait! Don't go, I should want Alex and I don't. We should hate each other but we don't and I have to think that all means something." With each word, she'd moved closer and now stood on the passenger side of my car. She came around the hood and leaned her forehead against my chest.

"We have two days left to homecoming

before you leave again and I want those two days." She cleared her throat. "With you."

I could've told her then about the job and what I wanted for our future, but she pressed her lips against mine and nothing mattered more than touching her and loving her. Some things never changed.

One Decade Ago

Every muscle and bone in my body ached. Practice was killing me and sleeping/not sleeping with Avery was about to finish the job. I loved holding her, loved when she turned toward me and held me, but she had no idea what *just* sleeping beside her was doing to me. I wanted her so bad, also didn't want to push her into anything she wasn't ready for. But oh God. I wanted her and it was killing me.

But as soon as I walked onto the boat, all my aches and pains subsided. And it was because of the rose petals. Red candles and the flower petals lined the path from the deck to the cabin and I followed. Because there was no force of nature or God strong enough to keep me from finding out what Avery had planned and if it was even close to what I hoped, I definitely wanted to see it with my own eyes.

When I walked into the cabin, she turned from the mirror and smiled. I, on the other hand, almost swallowed my tongue. Between the body, the lingerie, the candlelight flickering away the shadows on her skin, I was already hard and panting. But she looked so…beautiful, and I'd been dreaming of her for longer than we'd even been talking.

I couldn't move. I wanted to, I wanted to cross the room, lift her into my arms and take her to bed. But I couldn't. All communication between brain and body had ceased.

I stared at her. Took in the black nylons and garters. The red panties. And oh my, the red lace bra I could see through. I groaned I couldn't hold it in. But it was okay because I wanted her to know what she did to me, how much I wanted her, how beautiful she looked. I couldn't form a word to tell her, but I could groan, so I did.

"Cat got your tongue?" She had so much confidence as she walked toward me. "Naughty kitty. I'm gonna want you to have that back."

She traced the vein in my throat with her fingernail, scratching just enough to make my eyelids flutter and my breath hitch. If that wasn't enough, she pushed my shirt up and kissed my chest, paying special attention to each of my nipples and because I needed to hang onto something, I put a hand on each of her hips and aligned them with mine, drawing her close, grinding my needy body against hers.

Her gasp and the tension in her spine that made her straighten told me as much as anything she could've said. She needed to be in control. To set the pace and if it killed me, I would let her because I didn't want to stop this time. I didn't want to have to spend another night in a cold shower after she fell asleep.

She ran her hands down my arms then lifted them and stripped my shirt off. This woman had moves. Now our bodies were skin to skin, and I moaned when she rubbed against me and hitched her leg over my hips. I stayed still as long as I could, but there was too much Avery in the room for me to not react. I picked her up with a hand on each of her ass cheeks and her pussy cradled my dick, then carried her to the bed. As I laid her down, she kept her ankles locked around me and I covered her body with mine for a second, until I had to see her again, had to taste her skin.

The bra wasn't much more than two triangles of lace and a couple of strings with a tiny little satin tie in front. And since I was using my hands to hold myself up, I lowered my head to take the string between my teeth. I needed to shave and the hair of my face rasped against her skin as she used her leg strength to lift her hips and grind against my cock.

"Keaton..."

Oh God, nothing in the world sounded as perfect as the way she said my name. Nothing felt better than her body against me. Nothing tasted as sweet as her nipple in my mouth. I swirled my tongue, and she writhed again. When I bit down softly, she arched her back and ran her hand through my hair, holding my head against her breast.

My heart thumped like a big bass drum, and my dick strained against my pants, but I couldn't dare set it free yet. I wanted to make this good for her, so good she never wanted anyone else, and giving in to my dick right now would end this too quickly.

I sat up, and she whimpered until I disentangled her legs and pushed them apart then kissed my way down her body to her panties, delectable scraps of silk and lace, but they had to go. When she reached for me, I took her hands and laced our fingers together as I continued to kiss my way across her lower belly and down each thigh.

Her panting came harder, and I let go of one hand to graze her clit with the back of my finger. She arched her back and squeezed the hand still tangled with hers.

"Keaton." She whispered my name again, then moaned when I trailed my tongue over her panties. "Oh, baby."

And then… "Take my panties off. Lick my pussy."

Loud.

"Oh yes, baby."

I stuttered to a stop and she tensed again, then pulled away. I reached for her, but she twisted away. "Avery."

"That was wrong, wasn't it? Fucking porn." She shook her head, scowled, then sighed and covered her face with her hand.

And just when I thought my dick couldn't get any harder, she pulled out the porn card. "You watched porn?"

My palm itched to feel the weight of her breast. I curled my fingers into a fist.

She nodded. "I wanted to know what to expect. What you expected." She hid her face again, then turned away so that I had a nice view of her backside. I didn't want to scare her with my hard-on which was probably going to be a permanent fixture in my pants until the day I died, but I scooted closer to hold her and gasped when it rubbed against her ass.

"They always say, 'lick my pussy' and 'oh yeah, baby.' Always." Hearing her say it made me want to do it and my dick was to the point of pain it was so hard.

"Is that what you want me to do?" I kissed her shoulder and splayed my hand over her ribcage so that my thumb brushed the bottom of her breast.

"I don't know, all I know is, I'm

embarrassed." Her voice went thin, lost the huskiness of a moment ago. She buried her face in the pillow but kept her body aligned with mine and I let my hand drift a little higher.

Damn. I had to save this, for both of us. "I'm going to touch you, and if you want me to stop, you just say stop. No questions, no worries."

Fuck, I didn't want her to tell me to quit, especially when she let me circle her nipple with the pad of my index finger. She inhaled on a gasp and exhaled on a moan.

"Is that okay?" She nodded and I kissed her shoulder. "Good."

I let my hand slide along her stomach to the waistband of those delicious panties, then over the fabric covering her. There was no way I could touch her without coming in my damned pants, so I moved my hand to knead her thigh. She twisted, pushing me onto my back with her half on top of me, one leg thrown over my hip, the other as leverage against the bed while she ground her ass against my dick and guided my hand inside her panties.

Holy.

Fuck.

She was tight and wet, and I wanted her so bad I couldn't think. Especially when she moved to sit between my legs and pulled me up behind her. Holy shit. She'd moved the mirror to the end of the bed, and I could see us over her shoulder, my hand in her panties, hers pinching and twisting her nipples.

My dick throbbed against my zipper, but I wanted to give her everything. Every single fantasy she'd ever had. And it occurred to me right then and for the first time in my life, that she'd watched porn and I might not…measure up to her expectations. It wasn't enough to make my dick soft, but my brain stopped cooperating. Thank fuck she didn't have much experience to make a comparison.

I moved from behind her and smiled when she whimpered and reached for me. I walked around the edge of the bed and leaned over her to kiss her belly and slide my hands under her knees to pull her to the end of the bed with her lower legs hanging over.

"Take these off." I ran my knuckles over the panties, and she moaned and pulled the side ties at the same time and I yanked the fabric out from under her. I could see the moisture, wanted to taste her, wanted her to watch me. I pushed her legs apart wide and kissed the inside of each thigh while I trailed a finger from her clit down to her entrance and back up. When I couldn't stand it anymore, I let my tongue follow the same path while I slipped the tip of my finger inside her.

So tight, I almost came right then thinking of her pussy squeezing my cock. She laid back, and I lifted my head. "Watch me."

She leaned up on one elbow and threaded her fingers through my hair as I slid my tongue in and out of her then swiped upward.

"Keaton." She curled her fingers and

tugged my hair. "Should I come? Or should I… wait?" There wouldn't be any waiting. There would be moaning and screaming maybe, but not waiting. She tightened her thighs around my head and held me as she writhed and cried out, as I tasted the sweet, saltiness of her. "Oh shit! Oh, fuck! Oh shit!"

Definitely screaming, it was so hot, I couldn't take any more.

She relaxed her muscles, and I stood, shoved my pants away, and pulled the condom from my wallet. As soon as I rolled it on, I covered her body with mine. Desperate. So needy. So ready for her and she was ready for me. Or I thought so. But she closed her eyes and bit her lip.

"You okay?" I prayed she'd say yes. No way did I want to stop now.

She nodded, eyes still shut, fists clenched full of blanket now. "I'm nervous. This is…new to me."

She'd said she didn't have *as*

much experience. Not that she didn't have *any*. But that would explain why she'd had to use porn for research. She hadn't been trying to figure out what I might want, but about what *any guy* would want.

"New like brand new, tags still on? Or new like…got it at a yard sale so new to you but not brand new." My metaphors made zero sense, but my hard-on was deflating like an untied balloon.

"Well," she shrugged one naked shoulder, "I've dabbled." She closed her eyes. "You know, like a solo run."

She sighed and opened her eyes, looking everywhere but at me. "This is stupid. I'm a virgin. I mean, I've had orgasms before, not like that one, but you know…I just haven't wanted to…or been asked to…have sex with anyone."

Her face darkened, and I leaned down for a kiss because to not kiss her would've killed me. But as I moved in, she covered her face with her hands. I pulled one away, then the other.

The range of emotions running through me was intense, stark, and raw. I wanted her to know that she wasn't like every other girl I'd been with, that being with her meant something to me.

"Avery, will you make love with me?" Being with her made me wimpy, but I didn't mind, not for her.

She nodded and pulled me down for the kiss she'd just denied me. And I knew what heaven was all about when I inched inside of her and she clung to me until the pain subsided and she could enjoy our time together.

It wasn't a perfect night, but it was perfect for us. And it was the moment I knew I loved Avery Stroh more than anything in the world.

Chapter 19

Avery

I hadn't been so happy before in my life. So loved, so deliciously sore. I glanced up at Keaton who was staring at me. "What?"

"I was just thinking I don't want to get up."

It was only about five in the morning. "Then don't."

I dragged my knuckles down his stomach, and he caught my wrist in his hand before I got near the fun zone. He brought it up and kissed each of my fingertips then smiled, but it didn't reach his eyes. The little cynic in me started name-calling; heartbreaker, asshat, womanizer. But since we were on the short-term plan, not quite two days left, heartbreaker wasn't really fair. I hung onto asshat because any guy who walked out after doing what we'd just done was definitely an asshat.

"Okay, if we aren't going to have sex, do you want some breakfast?"

"I actually have some things to do this morning."

I faked a pout, but he didn't budge.

"And we're out of condoms anyway."

I grinned because grinning at him was one of the easiest things in the world and because if that was the worst of our problems, I could figure a work-around. "There's more than one way to skin a cat, you know."

He held his hand up to mine, sliding his palm back and forth, then lacing our fingers together. "I've never really understood that expression. Who the hell wants to skin a cat?"

"I think you're missing my point." I rolled closer and threw my leg over his. "My point is there are plenty of very exciting things we can do that don't require condoms." I pressed a kiss over his heart, then kissed his nipple with full tongue. "I don't want to waste the couple of days we have left."

He cleared his throat and sat up, pushing me aside, gently, but still moving me off him. "Actually, there's something we should talk about."

Uh-oh. I didn't like the sound of that. And the cynic was back to her old tricks....jerk, weasel, shit for brains, although the last one could have fit either of us. "Talk about?"

"Yeah." He rubbed his hands together then folded them in his lap. "It could be good news. Like for us. As a couple. I think." A bubble of worry closed around my heart as his brow wrinkled and he looked everywhere but at me. "After my last concussion, I really thought my football career was over, you know? Between the concussions and an almost negative passer rating, the sacks…not much chance I'll ever suit up for a game again. But…," he shook his head.

"Keaton. What are you saying?" I needed him to say it soon because my guts were twisting, and my brain was busy conjuring up reasons he was walking out on me early.

"Well, Rollins, the football coach here offered me a job as the QB coach."

Did that mean…? "Are you staying?"

The weight on my heart didn't lift but it lightened by a fraction. The smallest fraction possible. But if he was staying, there was a chance we could…be…more.

"I could. But then today, my agent called, and I've been released from the roster." He shook his head and shrugged as if he didn't care, but his gaze flickered and a flash of hurt passed through before he tried to smile and I laid a hand on his chest, hoping I could ease the pain from the outside.

It took a second for me to decipher all of his words. I didn't understand his use of 'but.' "That's great. So, you can take the job."

He nodded. "Except, the network also offered me a job in the booth, commentary, analysis."

He shook his head. "Pays a lot. But it's in Los Angeles."

"Oh. That's almost three thousand miles." All my dreams of us being together as more faded and he sighed. My stomach sank to my toes. "And it's the job you want?"

He didn't look at me.

"More than you want to stay here?" I didn't add the *with me* part. It would have killed me to hear the answer if it didn't go the way I wanted it to. "It's okay. It's your career, I get it."

I sat up and picked at a few pieces of imaginary lint on the blanket before I spoke again. "It's only football season, right?" That was me. Finding the bright side. Miss Glass Half Full.

"It's a little more than that, but..." he sighed. "I don't want to walk away from a future with you for a job I don't care about. But I don't want to stay if there's no future for us...if these last two days are all you want."

I wanted more, I wanted everything with him, and it was ridiculous considering our decade-plus of history consisted mostly of mistrust and silence.

"You shouldn't base your decision on me." I couldn't look at him even as he rested his chin on my shoulder and kissed the side of my throat. "I don't want you to..."

He curled his finger under my chin and urged me to face him. "Avery, I want you to be part of this, of my life, my decisions, my future. I don't want to lose you now. Not for a job or for anything else."

His voice was low and husky, sweet and deep.

And for one second, I basked in the glow of that happiness, that he wanted me to help him decide what to do, but then the pressure it put on our relationship crushed me. What if he stayed for me and we didn't work out? The chemistry was good between us, but if it faded, there was no other foundation for us to fall back on.

"So, what do you think? If you were picking right now."

With his finger rubbing a trail from my shoulder to wrist and his lips pressing soft slow kisses on my neck and jaw, I wanted him to stay, but I couldn't tell him that. It wasn't fair. And when my silence stretched longer than he apparently appreciated, he breathed out a scoff.

"Okay then." He pushed the blanket back. "I really do have to get going, I need to talk to the coach and call my agent."

He yanked his jeans up. "Then I have a thing at the Alpha house. So, I'll…" He cleared his throat. "I'll try to come by later, but if I don't make it, I'll see you tomorrow."

He grabbed but didn't put on his shirt or shoes before he raced out the door like his ass was on fire and there was a water trough in his front seat.

Good Lord. I really needed to work on my after-sex game because this wasn't the first time he'd shot out the door after.

One Decade Ago

Holy shit. Someone should've warned me about the emotional fallout of having sex for the first time. The pain had been intense for a couple seconds, but that wasn't why I was crying into his chest while he pretended to want to hold me. I couldn't be sure where the tears came from, actually, I only knew I couldn't turn them off.

And Keaton's wide eyes and half-parted lips every time I looked up at him said he didn't know what to do about it either.

"Are you okay?" He patted my shoulder, and I sobbed harder.

I just loved him so much. I didn't ever want to be without him again.

No. As soon as I had the thought, I kicked it away. "I don't love you."

"Okay. Good." He nodded, and my heart broke a little more.

Good? What the fuck did *good* mean? He was actually happy I didn't love him? What the fuck?

I couldn't stay here. "I have to go."

I stood, taking the blanket I had wrapped around myself, and headed to the stairs.

He tugged the tail of the blanket. "You live here."

I nodded. Yeah, I did. "Right. You should go."

He chuckled. "It's my dad's boat."

And we were back to me going. I jerked the tail of the comforter from his hand and when the top slipped into a wardrobe malfunction of the Janet Jackson variety as I reached for the door handle, I tugged it up which knocked off the entire rhythm of my dramatic departure. Before I could slide out onto the deck, Keaton put a hand on my shoulder. "What's going on?"

I had no idea, I could only think of one thing to explain it.

"I lied. I love you. So much." I shrugged. "And you said 'good' when I said I didn't, so I have to go now."

"You love me. Uh…" His eyes went wider, and he dropped his hands, then crossed them over his chest, then dropped them again. After a second of staring at his fingers, he punched a fist to his hip, then waved it around before pointing at me. "Thank you."

He nodded like a bobblehead doll. "I appreciate that, but I-I-I need-I need to get going. Football. Because I'm the quarterback. They can't play without me…so…I have to go to…practice."

He slid his legs into his jeans then tried with

a valiant amount of effort to slip his head through the armhole of his shirt before he gave up and yanked it off. "That's wrong. I'll just carry it."

His reaction to my spontaneous blurt of affection calmed me. It made me wonder what the hell I was thinking, and more, why my saying such a thing would make him act like I had a gun pointed at his penis. "Keaton?"

He nodded and cleared his throat again. "I'll call you. You know. Today. Later."

"Okay." Before I even had the word out of my mouth, he'd disappeared out the door, shoes in one hand, shirt in the other.

My heart shattered into a thousand pieces. I never should've said I loved him. I didn't love him, I couldn't be in love with him. We'd only known each other, really known each other a couple days. And we'd only slept together once. I mean, I wasn't an expert or anything, but I was pretty sure multiple orgasms still only counted as sleeping together once so long as we didn't leave the house between world rockings. But whether I came once or twice or four times, thank you very much, I certainly had enough sense to know that sex didn't equal love. That came from somewhere else and I'd used the word prematurely. By a year or two, at least and I'd scared him off. Sent him running, literally.

I would've never believed I would've turned into one of those girls who poured her heart out just because she'd spread her legs for some guy. But Keaton wasn't just some guy and to have "poured my heart out" would mean I really loved him…that wasn't possible either. Right?

I flopped backward on the bed and waited for the phone to ring.

Chapter 20

Keaton

Avery didn't make love like she didn't care, or maybe she fucked like she did care, I didn't know which way to look at it. All I knew was, Avery didn't feel the same way about me that I felt about her and maybe it wasn't fair to expect her to, but I did. I expected her to be as invested in us as I was, and when she wasn't, I wanted to die. My skin felt too tight, my head too clouded, and my guts too twisted for me to stay in a room and pretend I didn't care about her answer, or more specifically, her non-answer.

I wanted to stay with her, see where this thing between us ended up and I didn't need to see my face on TV to be a part of the game. Coaching put me on the field, with the team, every week. TV paid more, kept me relevant. But that didn't get me anything and it meant leaving Avery.

I walked into the Alpha house no clearer on a plan than I'd been after I talked to Avery. The house hadn't changed much. There were still four TVs in the living room, although they were bigger now, hanging on the walls and the wires for the attached game machines had been replaced by invisible blue tooth connections. There were guys sprawled on the four leather sofas, some playing those video games, some lounging to watch game footage, and in the middle of it all, Ryder and Finn.

Finn looked up when he saw me, but Ryder tossed his controller to one of the younger guys, then walked three steps toward me. I wasn't really in the mood to deal with this shit, but neither was I in the mood to brawl with someone who didn't fight fair.

"Keaton!" I didn't mistake his tone for happiness to see me. He only sounded jubilant to those who didn't know him as I did. To me, he sounded bitter and angry.

He slapped me on the back like we hadn't just seen each other a couple days ago like we were still friends, and there was a time we were. That time had passed. Now, I didn't know what we were. "Let's have a drink and catch up on old times."

He led me to the kitchen with his arm still slung around my neck. Once we each had a beer in hand, he leaned against the counter and looked me up and down.

"How you been, Ryder?"

He laughed and tipped his beer back, just two guys having a drink and a chat. But so much more simmered under the surface and we were bubbling, about to explode all over the laminate floor.

"Now you care?" His eyes flashed, and my entire body tensed, on alert, ready for the first blow, but then he laughed. "I'm a secretary now. Working my way up in Dad's company."

All his big dreams went down the toilet the minute he got kicked out of school. There was supposed to be a football career, then a job with his dad. But after the Glouster scandal went nationwide, no one would touch him.

I didn't know what to say to that, I knew why he was bitter. Guys like Ryder only assigned blame for their faults, never took it. But I didn't have to talk because he kept going.

"Things turned out good for you, though, you got the contract, the lifestyle, everything we wanted." His voice turned hard and angry. "And the girl, too. But you always got the girl." He smacked his hand against the butcher block twice. "You got everything. Always."

"Yeah right, I got my face and my dick all

over the internet." I hadn't quite reached the forgive and forget part of our relationship and the meltdown was coming. I set my beer down, and he smacked it away so that it shattered against the far wall.

This wasn't our space anymore, we didn't even belong here and now we were drawing a crowd. Ryder always played to the crowd. He looked at the couple guys standing in the doorway. "This guy is a legend, fucked more girls in this house than all the rest of us combined."

He walked around the table to sling his arm around my neck and pull me down so that our heads knocked together. I shoved his chest, and he let go. "Should've seen this guy, he didn't even need lines. Just that pretty face and his big dick, girls were dying to get in here."

My skin burned as the crowd grew.

"And we have all the home movies, don't we, buddy?" He shot me a wink.

Oh, shit....he chuckled, and I hated him

because this was going to end badly. For me, for the Alpha house, and for Ryder. "Don't do this, Ryder."

He stared at me with his wide-open, angry eyes and a grim line for a mouth. "Cops let you go once. They won't do it again."

I didn't even know if that was true, but I'd almost lost everything right along with him and I couldn't risk that again. Couldn't risk losing Avery after we'd just started figuring things out and I could see a future with her in it.

He laughed. "I'm not the star of the show. I'm not even here right now. I wasn't invited back to celebrate the centennial of the fraternity I ran."

He had a point, he hadn't been asked back, which begged the question…what the fuck was he doing there? He blamed me for what happened to him because I was the only one who hadn't been kicked out of school. Of course, I was also the only one who wasn't in on it.

One Bet

He'd used me, set up his whole operation using his "secret" video recordings to blackmail some of the girls into working for him, to humiliate others, and the videos he couldn't use, he sold. The cops had gotten them back, as far as I knew. I hadn't shown up on any porn sites that I'd ever been able to find so I'd stopped looking, but maybe he'd restarted his little entrepreneurial enterprise and neglected to mention it.

His dad paid off all the girls to keep quiet, except Avery. She hadn't taken a dime, and she'd pressed charges. But by then, the damage had been done. She'd believed I knew about it all, that I was in on it with Ryder.

I should've known when the fallout started happening, that Ryder was going to try to take us all down with him, but he'd been my best friend since he'd come to Dallas stadium for football camp when he was a senior in high school, I'd trusted him.

· · ·

A Decade Ago

Ryder fidgeted in the chair next to me, he looked at me then away, then looked at me again.

Jameson nudged me. "We're screwed."

Maybe, not that I could say why, not that I had a single clue why I'd been hauled into the dean's office with Ryder, Jameson, and Finn. "Why?"

Finn leaned around Jameson to stare at me. "Obviously, they have one of the videos."

"Videos. Right." Videos of what?

Finn chuckled. "God, it's a good thing you're a rockstar on the gridiron because you're an idiot."

Finn and I weren't as tight as me and Ryder, but I'd always thought we were friends. Why the fuck was he insulting me now?

"It must be because I don't have a fucking

clue what we're doing here." I stared at Finn, then Jameson, and finally, Ryder. No one answered or offered up any information, so I had no choice but to wait until the dean walked in and slid behind her desk.

Dean Ferguson stared at us as a group then each one individually. Her long blonde hair was piled on top of her head and she wore a business suit and an expression that said this wasn't a meeting to praise our good grades or our school spirit.

My stomach churned. I'd never even been called into the principal's office. She opened her laptop and after a few quick keystrokes, turned the screen to face us. In living color, there I was, hands on her hips while a very naked and very loud Sheri Epson rode my dick in my room at the Alpha house.

I hadn't filmed a video and I sure as hell never invited anyone into my room to take a video. I glanced at Ryder who had the good grace to stare down at his hands, and the misfortune of not being able to control his smirk. Finn stared out the window, and Jameson nodded at me. I was the only one surprised by what was on the screen.

"The university has received a complaint signed by three women whose similar videos have been found online." Dean Ferguson sighed and closed then turned the laptop away and folded her hands on top of the machine. "Mr. Shaw, as costar of each video, I'm allowing you to explain yourself."

I couldn't believe this. My friends had taped me? And uploaded it to the web? I glanced at each one of them again. "What did you do?"

Finn raised his eyebrows and nodded to Ryder, but that couldn't be right. He wouldn't... And our friendship meant nothing. I stood, Ryder, Finn, and Jameson stood, and I shoved Ryder against the wall behind us. I held him there with an arm against his throat. "You son of a bitch. What the fuck did you do?"

He laughed and pushed me off, I backed

away because of our friendship.

"Keats, you worry way too much, these chicks aren't going to do anything. The school isn't going to do anything." He straightened his shirt. "We take down the videos and throw some money at them and it all goes away. Or the donations that come from Kennedy and Associates will all dry up and Dean Ferguson knows it. That's the beauty of running a private university, right? A private university that's dependent on our ridiculous tuition and donations from people like *our* fathers." I couldn't process everything. Couldn't wrap my brain around what he was saying...but he kept saying it.

Dean Ferguson stood, braced her hands on her desk. "It's out of my hands, Mr. Kennedy." She cocked an eyebrow. "The complaint didn't come to the university from the young ladies. It came from the police department." Fuck. "And they have witnesses."

She sat down. "Pending our own

investigation that is going to run alongside that of the Maine State Police and the FBI, you're all suspended."

My stomach dropped. *Suspended*, for having sex. They were suspended for taping me having sex. All of my career plans, playing pro ball, becoming something more than the great Julian's little brother shriveled and died.

"You guys taped me?"

Ryder rolled his eyes and I wanted to kill him, rage shot through me in bursts. Jameson moved forward. "Keaton didn't know. Ryder set up the cameras, Finn operated the recorder, and Ryder and I made the deals."

Ryder lunged and Jameson fought him off with a fist that caught Ryder in the jaw and knocked him backward. "Keaton didn't know anything."

The dean looked at Finn. "Is that true?"

Finn smiled. "I want a lawyer."

Jameson ran his hands through his hair. "Ask your witnesses, they won't have anything on Keaton."

I appreciated his honesty, but I still wanted to kill him. To kill the three of them and anyone else who might've been involved. Holy fuck.

"Why me?" I looked at each of them. "You guys get laid as much as I do."

Not like they could answer in front of the dean without incriminating themselves. Well, not Ryder or Finn anyway. But Jameson had already admitted his part in this shit. He nodded. "True, but your videos were better and longer." He shrugged. "And with girls that everybody wanted to see."

"Deals with who?" Ferguson kept her voice calm, quiet, but the threat was real. Our futures were at stake and she knew it.

Jameson looked down.

"We made deals with the girls who wanted to keep making money." They were pimping out these girls? "And the guy who buys the videos."

"You fucking sold the videos?" Oh, fuck me

sideways. The damage they'd done, not just to me, but to the girls I'd been with, couldn't even be measured. My hands were shaking, and I couldn't stand any longer. I sank to my chair and buried my head in my hands.

"The police are waiting to speak with all of you." Dean Ferguson hit a button on her desk phone, and the door swung open beside Ryder, who now lounged against the wall as if he didn't have a care in the world.

I expected uniforms and guns drawn, but these guys wore suits and flashed FBI badges. The gravity of the situation weighed on me, this wasn't something anyone was going to be able to buy their way out of. Even if our money could speak for us, no way my dad would buy me out of anything anyway. I had to hope Jameson continued telling the truth and didn't try to save his own ass at my expense.

Three hours later, I was free. I had no information about the money or the videos, and I'd given them permission to search my room at the Alpha house, to download all the data from my phone. I'd also handed over my laptop and every other piece of electronic equipment I owned, from video games to a tablet to my iPod and the GPS in my car.

The guys lawyered up, except Jameson who made a deal to avoid prosecution and stay at Glouster. It took me another hour after my release to thank God that I'd never taken Avery back to my room. We were on shaky enough ground that I didn't think we would survive a scandal. It was at that moment I realized losing her would break me in ways I would never recover from. I also realized I loved Avery Stroh and now it was time to tell her everything.

Chapter 21

Avery

Déjà vu....the sensation of having already experienced the present situation. I'd spent an entire day trying to outthink it, outrun it, forget the reason why this felt so familiar.

And it was my own fault, I'd driven to the Alpha house, parked out front, watched as a fistfight spilled out into the front yard, Ryder and Keaton pounding each other, fist for fist, grunt for grunt. I'd seen this happen before, I'd been a little drunker, a little angrier, and a little sicker to my stomach, but it was the same scene ten years later.

As a member of the faculty, I should've stepped from the car, called campus police, and done whatever I needed to for student safety. Instead, I closed my eyes and heard Ryder's voice in my head.

"A bet's a bet, so here's your money. You earned it. If you ask me, you deserve a lot more for fucking that one."

I'd lived that moment, watched everyone at that party watch me and Keaton together. Listened as people commented about my lack of tits and laughed at my inexperience, howled at me.

I stopped remembering and lifted my head to watch Keaton and Ryder roll around on the grass while a couple of younger guys tried to pull them apart and because of the déjà vu, or maybe because I couldn't separate the man he'd become from the boy who'd broken my heart, I drove away.

I didn't want to go home. My house was still too full of his presence. I wasn't even there, and I could picture him standing against the kitchen counter with his cup of coffee and his bare chest. All I had to do was close my eyes to see him in the bathroom, brushing his teeth with a towel wrapped around his waist, or smiling down just before he kissed me.

My fingertips brushed my lips and I drove until I ran out of road and ended up at the marina. There were fourteen boat slips, but I only looked at number three. Once upon a time, there'd been a dreamboat parked between those two small docks. I'd fallen in love on that boat and had my heart broken there, too.

Now it was gone, hauled somewhere down the coast after the fire when it showed up on TV being searched by the cops. I sat staring at the water and that damned boat slip until the sun peeked over the ocean. Then I drove home, remembering everything that happened back then, exhausted and sad, more so because of

Ryder's appearance on campus. History was on a crash course to repeat itself.

One Decade Ago

I took a last look at the boat and walked down the dock. I'd already messed everything up with Keaton by telling him I loved him, and moving in with Alex was risky because there was no telling what stupid thing I would end up saying to ruin that friendship, but I couldn't stay on the boat, and Alex offered the piece of floor next to his bed.

His house was on the other side of town. After I called a cab to take me, I realized it was twelve dollars I didn't really have, but no way could I walk it while I was carrying the last of my worldly possessions and my broken heart.

But when we drove past the Alpha house, I tapped the driver on the shoulder. "Stop. Wait."

As he pulled the car close to the curb, I

stared at the scene unfolding in front of the house. Ryder and Keaton were trading punches while their friends whooped and howled. I climbed out and headed straight into the fray in time to duck one wayward fist and be caught by another.

I might have been voted the girl most likely to cut a guy, but it was just an act. First, I didn't like knives or guns or weapons of any kind, I liked peace and love and I hated blood. Especially when it was seeping from my lower lip, but I'd just been punched in the face and I wanted to kick a little ass. Ryder ass. But from my position, on my knees in front of him, I couldn't reach more than his dick, and so I punched where I could reach and he went down.

"Avery." Keaton's breath came in hard puffs as he wiped his mouth and crouched in front of me. "Are you okay?"

I shoved his hands away and brushed the dirt off my ass as I stood. Ryder, still on his side holding his balls, spat at the ground. "Bitch."

I lunged, foot drawn back and Keaton pulled me away. "Woah, Rocky."

This time I jerked away from him and crossed my arms. "Why are you guys fighting?"

Keaton glanced at Ryder who was making his way to his feet.

"It's nothing. Don't worry about it." He turned me toward the street. "Let's get out of here."

My cab still sat at the edge of the yard, and I remained a step ahead of him as we walked toward it. He climbed in behind me and leaned his head against mine, then sat up.

"Why's your stuff packed?" I didn't answer. "Avery, where you going?"

"I'm going to stay with Alex for a while. Until I can afford a place."

His eyes flickered and his lips parted. "You're leaving the boat? Is it because I didn't say I love you this morning?"

He shook his head.

"Avery..." He looked down. "Shit."

And I chuckled not because it was funny, but because I had a headache from being punched, and because it was either laugh or cry and there was no way was I crying in front of him, not again. "It's okay, you don't have to say it, I don't expect it. I just don't want it to be awkward between us, and staying at Alex's makes sense."

He shook his head. "No. It doesn't."

But the driver pulled up in front of Alex's building. I reached to open the door, and Keaton put a hand on my shoulder. "I love you, Avery. I do. I was scared this morning because I thought it was too fast, but I know you better than any girl I've ever dated."

I rolled my eyes. "That isn't saying much, Keaton."

"I know, but I want to be with you." He took my hand in his and brought it to his cheek. "And I do love you."

I shook my head and he held my hand to the side of his bruised face. "I'll say it a hundred times or a thousand. I'll say it until you believe me. I love you."

I didn't answer.

"I love you."

"Keaton." I didn't want pity I love yous. I wanted something deep and meaningful, not something I forced.

"I love you." When I sighed, he leaned his forehead against mine. "Please, Avery. I love you. I swear it. There's no one else I want to be with, no one I want to kiss or hold or love. Please come back to the boat with me."

When I turned to look at him, he tilted his head and a tear slid down his cheek. I didn't have any grand illusions about life, or ideals that made me more or less than anyone else. I also knew he could probably turn his tears on and off like a faucet if he needed to, but that one tear sealed my fate. I leaned over the seat to speak with the driver. "Could you take us back to the marina?"

By morning, I'd forgotten everything else except how Keaton Shaw took me in his arms, first in the back of that cab then later after we made love on the boat and said he loved me. Over and over he'd told me, and over and over I said it back. I'd been naïve enough to think love was enough and the future would work itself out.

Chapter 22

Keaton

Avery stayed away until dawn. I knew because I sat on her porch waiting, watching the light breeze stir the branches on the maple tree in her yard, counting the stars and the hours, hoping I could see her one last time since the job offer here would likely be retracted as soon as the administration got word of my most recent fistfight with Ryder.

She pulled her car in front of the cottage and stared at me for a couple of seconds before she opened the door and walked toward me. She waited until she stood at the bottom of her porch steps before she shook her head. "What are you doing here?"

I wanted to be honest with her. To tell her how badly I wanted to be with her. Instead, I smiled. "I missed you."

She didn't walk past me, but sat beside me, looking out at her yard, which needed to be mowed. After a silent minute, she turned her body toward mine and ran her hand down my cheek. "I know what you wanted me to say yesterday, that I want you to stay, that I want us to be...more." Neither the words nor the tone she used inspired visions of happily ever after and then there was the long, slow sigh.

"I would love for you to stay, for you to be... in the same state at least" she smiled but it was the saddest thing I'd ever seen. "On the same coast, maybe, but the job in Los Angeles is...I can't ask you to give that up for me."

She paused, again. "I think you should take it."

And now, because of my fight with Ryder, my choices were limited. "Why?"

She sighed. "I saw you with Ryder. Fighting." I didn't read her expression as disappointment as much as admiration and it made me smile. If anyone deserved to hit Ryder, it was Avery. I couldn't really blame her for the grin if the thought of punching him again gave her that satisfied look. After a second, she let out a slow breath. "What's he doing here anyway?"

She deserved to know, but I didn't have any idea beyond the fact it would be something shady and quite possibly illegal.

"I don't know." I wished I did.

Ryder's motives weren't something I could guess, but it didn't take a genius to figure it wouldn't be good. In his mind, transparent as it was, he had plenty of reason to be angry. At me, at Avery, at anyone who'd spoken against him. Which also put Jameson and Finn on the block. But right now, I couldn't worry about anyone but Avery.

She shook her head and waved a hand. "Unless he's up to try his hand at murder, there isn't much he can do to hurt me now."

Murder? The word sliced through me with all its implications. "He's too chicken shit for jail and I don't think his daddy would be able to buy him out of it if he kills someone." The way he had with the situation ten years ago. And if he hurt Avery, there was no way he'd live long enough to go to trial. "Chances are, he's going to go after me and not you."

Unless he happened to remember the way to cause the sharpest pain for me would be to go after Avery and I should've told her just so she could be prepared, but I didn't want to give her an excuse to make me go away. I didn't want her to protect herself by throwing up a wall between the two of us. This time, I would be the one to protect her.

One Bet

. . .

One Decade Ago

I couldn't wait to find Avery, couldn't wait to tell her about my day, the contract offer, the agent, the money. She'd be mad my meeting went long, madder still I was late meeting her, but it was our way out of here. Our future…

Someone handed me a beer, someone else pushed me down the hallway and into Ryder's room. He handed me a wad of cash. "Bad news, bud. Sigmas won't have her. Said they prefer to take the trash out not let it pledge, but a bet's a bet, so here's the money I owe you. You earned it, if you ask me, you deserve a lot more for fucking that one."

I wanted to punch him for talking about Avery that way. Instead, I shoved my hand and his money against his chest. And then he laughed.

A second later the hooting began. "Lick my

pussy, Keaton." The voice, Avery's voice, came from the living room. Through speakers turned at top volume.

I wheeled around through the kitchen, then into the living room where an image of Avery, naked and more than life-size, on her knees while I pounded into her from behind, played on the four TVs simultaneously. Someone howled, then someone else howled and it took about three seconds before everyone in the room except Avery was making fun of the video. Avery stood, mouth open, tears streaming down her cheeks until she turned and ran out.

Ryder chuckled behind me. "Always best to go out on a high note. I think this was the best video yet."

I drove my fist into his jaw and dove on top of him when he fell backward. The satisfying crunch of his face under my knuckles didn't calm me down much, didn't take away the feeling of loss, didn't make me want him dead any less. Someone pulled me off and dragged me outside.

I shoved away the hands holding me. "Get off me."

Finn yanked me back when I went back for the door.

"Keaton, stop!" He moved to stand in front of me. Bigger. Sturdier. Could have probably bench-pressed me with one hand. No way was I going through him, or around him since he was quick for a big guy. "You can't go after him. For her sake."

He shook his head. "Think about it. He's already gone after Jameson and me."

Jameson had ended up in the hospital after practice today from a bad hit he took from Ryder. "And now he's used her to get to you, don't let him get you kicked out of school."

I flexed my hand and shook my head. "I'm leaving school anyway."

Finn frowned. "You don't have to. Mr.

Kennedy took care of everything. We're all covered."

I was covered anyway because I was innocent, and I didn't give a fuck about anyone but Avery. I had to get to her, had to make sure she was okay.

By the time I got to the boat, she was standing on the dock, arms folded at her waist while she watched the boat burn.

"Avery?" I didn't care if she'd set the damned thing on fire, just that she was okay.

She turned, held out her hand as if to ward me off, and backed up a couple of steps. "Get away from me."

"Avery...I didn't know he taped us." I moved a little closer and she jerked a little further away, hand still extended between us.

"Well, how the hell else would you prove you won *the bet*?"

Oh no.

"Avery, let me explain. Please." When she

shuffled around me, I reached out to grab her, I just wanted her to stay, to listen.

And she stopped walking but looked down at the spot where I held her arm. "Get your hands off me, or I swear to God, you're going to need a surgeon to sew your fucking fingers back on."

"Avery, please don't go." But she walked past me, down the dock and away, and until the next morning, I thought maybe she would give me a chance to tell her all of it. I'd also hoped she would forgive me. But by the time the sun came up and the school's blog was published, I knew it was over.

Chapter 23

Avery

Maybe it was lack of sleep or the fact Keaton Shaw took up all the oxygen in my house, but I couldn't form a cohesive thought. I hoped he would stay even though I knew it was unlikely. I wanted him to take me in his arms even though I knew there was only hurt on the other side of this day.

But when he stood and pulled me into his arms, kissed me until I couldn't breathe, nothing else mattered. Not that Ryder was in town or the Susie/Alex issue or the fact Keaton was probably leaving, I didn't care.

I cared about his arms around me, his lips urging mine apart, the hand he had braced between my shoulder blades, the way he let me lead us backward until I was pressed between his body and the wall. He pulled me close to him, then lifted me so I could grind against his hard cock. If that wasn't why he lifted me, I didn't care. Need thrummed through every cell and vein in my body, the need to feel his skin, to find a release for the building pressure, to kiss more of him.

The shadow of his beard rasped against my throat when he kissed my jaw then took my earlobe between his teeth. I could feel the evidence of his wanting me without his warm breath on my ear, but the sensation along with the words went straight to my panties. I locked my legs around him and ground against him, driving my fingers into his hair while he wrapped his hand around my thigh then brushed his fingers against my pussy.

I put my legs down and used my body to push him toward the back onto the table. Desperation gave me grace and fluidity I didn't have without it and I used the chair to climb on top of him. The table came with the cottage so I couldn't be sure it would hold us, but damned sure we were going to give it a try. I didn't have time for a stroll through the house to the sofa or to the bedroom, I needed him right now.

He reached up to kiss me, but I put a hand on his chest and held him down while I gyrated, and his breath caught. I wanted to taste him and fuck him and be tasted and be fucked by him and I wanted it all right now. He pushed his hands under my sweater and shoved my bra up then pinched my nipples until my pussy tightened and I moaned. Nothing felt as good as Keaton between my legs with his hands on my body.

I tugged his shirt free from his pants and

yanked the buttons open. Holy hell, this man had a chest and stomach that made me want to kiss every square inch of his skin. Instead, I ran my hands from his throat to his waistband and attacked the button and zipper on his jeans. He gasped as I yanked away his boxers then stroked him as I slid away and used my free hand to strip off my clothes.

"Fuck, I love it when you touch me, Avery." His voice was low, husky, sexy, and my body vibrated as he reached for me and his eyes raked over me as physical as any touch. My skin heated but I continued to stroke him, to watch his face as his eyelids fluttered and an easy smile turned his lips. "Come here."

I wanted more than to climb on and ride him, but I couldn't wait another minute to feel him inside me, to lower myself onto him, to throw my head back and lose myself in every sensation that came along with making love with Keaton.

He thrust and I moaned, the table creaked

and I moaned. He pulled me down so we were chest to chest and mouth to mouth and I moaned. Then he arched up, kissed my breasts, and held me while we rocked, and the table threatened with more creaking and a few groans of its own as Keaton shifted so his thrusts came harder and faster and I could meet each one with an answer.

I wanted more, so much more. Enough that if he left to go to Los Angeles, I would have a memory to keep me warm until I figured out how to go back to living without him. He held me with one arm and braced himself with the other then drove into me until I couldn't think anymore, couldn't do more than gasp and hang on, and still he kept going. My world spun apart, and I could only see Keaton and feel Keaton, want him, breathe his name. "I love you."

It wasn't until I was back in the room, until the stars in my eyes faded that I realized what I'd said and tried to hide my face. Keaton pulled back so his shoulder no longer provided the security and protection from his gaze. "I love you, too."

Maybe I always had, I just wished I could stop saying it at moments like this.

He leaned his forehead against mine and brushed his finger down from my temple to my jaw then across to my chin.

"If you don't want to come with me to California, that's fine. I'll move here." He grinned. "I just don't want to let you go again."

And while I liked those words and loved the sentiment behind them, we hadn't been strong enough ten years ago to survive Ryder Kennedy. And we had less of a foundation to build on now.

One Decade Ago

Flames licked the side of the boat and smoke billowed up into the night sky as the Coast

Guard sprayed the fire from the oceanside and Department Three of the Glouster Maine volunteer fire services unit hosed it from the landside.

I was on the beach, they would come for me soon enough, know what I'd done, arrest me, and never believe it was an accident. The timing was too coincidental and maybe subconsciously, I'd done it on purpose. After all, if the boat was gone, the memory of my time with Keaton would be gone along with it. That was what I told myself as I sat crying as the ocean lapped at the beach.

"Hey. You okay?" Susie Chastain sat beside me on the beach and we watched Keaton's beautiful yacht sinking.

To be honest, I was numb, as if I'd watched the entire night happen to someone else. I nodded, but there was something I had to know, something I'd never wanted to ask that was as important to me now as it was to breathe. "Was it Keaton? Is he the one who hurt you?"

She inhaled slowly and exhaled loudly through her nose. "Not directly. But they're all alike, aren't they? Ryder, Keaton, Finn, and all the rest. They all think they can do whatever they want. Hurt whoever they want. Like we don't matter. Ryder did it to me, Keaton did it to you." She tossed a handful of sand in front of her then picked up another and threw it toward the waves. "We should expose them for the bastards they are."

"Yeah." But my heart wasn't in it. I'd lost everything from my place to stay to every stitch of clothing I owned, my books, my homework…to my boyfriend.

She tilted her head.

"I'm serious. We should…" She grabbed my hand. "Come on. I know what to do."

I went with her because I didn't have anywhere else to go, but I sat in her mom's living room and told our story, just the way it happened. Then I went to Alex's house. Alex, the editor of the school blog and newspaper, and I begged him to post it. Then, when he said yes, I kissed him, pretended he was the one I loved, pretended my heart wasn't broken and I could be happy knowing I'd gotten my revenge and revenge for all the girls whose names Susie supplied, and there'd been a lot of them.

Chapter 24

Keaton

I'd been to a hundred and one awkward dinners. Sit-downs where no one spoke or if they did the conversation remained stilted and choppy. I'd expected nothing more tonight, but so far, through appetizers and drinks, a relaxed atmosphere had settled over the room. Unless I counted Avery's fingernails digging into my hand every time Susie touched Jameson or kissed him or laughed at something he said.

The house was nicer than I expected for a

guy who worked as a freelance driver. The front was all brick with a wrap-around porch, but the inside was a testament to family and children. A bucket of toys sat in the corner next to a big screen with two different game systems underneath. Family pictures hung on every available wall space and sat on the tables. The walls were a brownish-gray trimmed in white and the staircase between the living room and dining room had even more photos of Jameson and Susie and their kids hanging in an angular formation leading up to the second floor.

Avery picked up one of the pictures from the side table, Susie in a long white dress and Jameson wrapped around her as she looked at the camera and he gazed so lovingly at her. The traditional tuxedo-veil-sunny day combo made them look even happier than their smiles would have shown. "So, you guys have been married a long time."

Susie narrowed her eyes. "Nine years last month."

She stood and went to the fireplace mantle to run her finger along the framed picture of a little boy in a soccer uniform. "This is our son Gabriel. He's eight."

She pointed to two little girls. "That's Amy and Jessica."

She replaced the picture Avery handed back then smiled at Jameson who handed me another beer. "We have so much to be thankful for."

Avery nodded.

"I see that." She smiled. "You've come a long way from painting graffiti, Susie."

Jameson nudged my shoulder. "I gotta start the grill. You want to see the backyard?" He'd never been subtle, but I appreciated the easy out. The appeal of watching Avery play tit for tat with Susie dimmed. Maybe I was jealous because she was defending a man who'd just told her he loved her. Or maybe I was just tired. Either way, a bit of fresh air sounded divine.

"Yeah." I followed him out a set of French doors. "You have a great house, Jameson."

He opened the lid to the grill then turned to look up at the second floor. "Yeah. Susie's making big money, she travels a lot and spends more time away than she spends here."

He turned back to the grill and sighed. "And you and Avery are here about Alex, right?" He looked down at his hands. "Not everything is what it seems."

He turned back to the grill and twisted a knob. "Avery's probably jumping up and down for joy thinking my wife is screwing around right under my nose, but I love my wife."

My heart ached for him, but it ached for me, too. In college, we'd been on top of the world, then, it all went to shit. Not that he hadn't played his part and me mine, but we'd fallen, crashed from our pedestals, and still had the scars to prove it.

He turned. "I'm a washed-up college football star who has a bum knee, got kicked out of college, and drives drunk people around in my car for a living. Where am I going to go?"

And I was a washed-up pro football player who had somehow managed to fall in love with a woman who'd tried to destroy me and I couldn't face the reality of it, so I changed the subject, quickly. "The university offered me a job as QB coach for the team."

He nodded, still the kind of guy who appreciated the good fortune of others more than he lamented his own lot in life. "That's great, man."

"Even more great, I get to pick my own staff. And I thought maybe you…"

He chuckled and held up his hand. "I have soccer practice with Gabe two nights a week. Ballet for Amy on Wednesday, piano and guitar with Jesse on Monday and Friday. School lunches have to be packed every night, baths, homework and I drive days and weekends. I don't know how I'd squeeze in two-a-day practices, traveling to other schools, workouts, and team meetings. I'd love to do it, but I don't see how I'd manage. I can't let my kids down, they're the one thing I do well."

And speaking of the little ones. "Where are your kids?"

"At my mom's." He shrugged and chuckled. "I wanted a grown-up night."

I would've told him that grown-up nights were over-rated but shouting from inside interrupted my thoughts.

Jameson burst through the door as Avery and Susie stood on opposite sides of the kitchen island. Avery was shaking her phone at Susie who had both hands braced on the wooden cutting board in the center of the room.

"This is none of your business." Susie hissed the words at Avery in a much quieter tone than we'd heard from the deck.

"He *is* my business." Jameson might have known about Susie's extracurricular boyfriend, but having it thrown in his face wasn't likely to keep the volatility under his surface from bubbling over.

I couldn't let her add to whatever Jameson was feeling right then. Something close to humiliation, I imagined. I moved to take Avery by the arm.

"We should go." I'd thought she would fight me, would pull away, but she didn't. She allowed me to lead her out. At the door, I looked back at Jameson. "Hey, the offer stands. If you can work it out, let me know."

He nodded and Avery and I walked out. I waited until we were in the car before I turned to her. "What did you think you were doing?"

"Protecting my friend." She spat the words and crossed her arms. "And I wasn't done yet."

"Jameson knows, okay? He knows about her and Alex."

But her eyes flashed. "I don't care about Jameson."

And maybe it was because being around Jameson made the memory of her article fresher, or maybe because I'd seen honest pain in my friend's face when he talked about his wife, or maybe because I didn't like this part of her, I shook my head. "I do care about him. And once again you have your facts all mixed up."

"My facts are fine, Jameson knowing that his wife is cheating is good. I'm glad he knows. But Alex doesn't know she's married and he deserves to know."

I didn't have a real reason for arguing with her except I was angry, and I didn't quite understand the depths of why. "How do you know he doesn't know?"

Maybe if she had something based on facts, but all she had were assumptions. It was reasonable to think Alex didn't know but considering Jameson had known about him it was equally reasonable to think Alex might know about Jameson.

"Because I know Alex and he wouldn't screw a married chick."

Obviously, she didn't know Alex as well as

she thought. "You didn't know he was seeing her and you didn't know he was in love with you."

She shook her head and pursed her lips. There was nothing I could say to counter her decisiveness. "He deserves the truth."

I stared at her. "The truth or your version?" I wasn't accusing her of making anything up, just a skewed perspective. Right now I just needed to think this through away from her.

I started the car and drove toward her house.

"What the hell does that mean?"

It meant I was angry, angrier than I'd ever realized because she didn't understand that not everything was black and white. I'd been guilty of treating all those women badly in college. I hadn't taken the videos or sold them, or used them for blackmail, but if not for me, there wouldn't have been any women to exploit and Jameson had been wrapped up in the dark side of it, but in the end, he'd done what he could to make it right. He'd come forward and given the facts to the cops, paid a fine he couldn't afford, lost his parents' support, his chance to graduate with an education, and his future from the scandal. How much more did he have to pay? But I wanted her to see it on her own, and it disappointed me that she didn't. "If you don't know, you won't understand when I explain it."

She scoffed. "I don't know, I'm pretty smart. Try me."

When I didn't speak further because I didn't want to say anything I would regret, she twisted toward the window.

"Fine." After a minute, she turned back to me. "Please tell me what you meant."

I wanted the words to make sense, to not be led with emotion, but we'd never dealt with any of it. After the party, she'd stopped talking to me, and I'd let her because I felt guilty for all of it. My friend hurt her and he used me to do it, the cops got involved, Ryder and Finn got kicked out of the fraternity and then school, and Jameson, who'd already withdrawn because of his injury, was told he couldn't return. Then the article came out.

"Instead of talking to me, or taking your case to the dean, you went after us publicly so that the school didn't have any choice but to get rid of us. You hid behind that article and you didn't care that Jameson defended me. He told the truth and still, you went after him and me. I was completely innocent, I didn't even know until we got called into the dean's office." There were so many things about the whole situation that she'd had wrong and as fucked up as what Ryder did was, he'd saved my contract and confessed to everything. By then, the scandal had spread too far, national news and Finn lost his scholarship, his chance at playing professionally, and he'd left for Europe.

"I didn't hide behind anything. I wrote what happened and the consequences fit the crime."

"You wrote what you heard, what you saw, what he did. Then you refused to talk to me about my part in it even after the cops cleared me."

The more I pointed out her part in it all, the sadder I got. Neither of us was the people we'd been back then, but now we would only be constant reminders of what those people had done and I didn't know if it was something we could get over.

"I wrote what happened to me and to Susie and to all the other girls who believed they were something special and you're far from innocent. I loved you and you destroyed me, but you won your bet, right? So, it's all good." She held up her hand. "You know what? I don't want to have this fight. It was a long time ago, I'd rather forget it and move on."

She was right, we both needed to forget it and together we never would.

"I think this is always going to be between us." There. I'd said it.

She stared at me as I glanced between her and the road. "What are you saying?"

What was I saying? "I'm saying there's a lot of feeling and emotion we didn't work through because you wouldn't talk to me."

She nodded. "I'm sorry I didn't kiss it all better for you, Keaton. I'm sorry I was hurt and angry and too humiliated to see how much this affected *you*."

I pulled the car in front of her house and switched the ignition off. I didn't want this to be the end of us, but I wanted us to figure out how to live with what happened so we could go on. Together.

I opened my door, but she turned. "Don't bother. I can see myself inside."

I didn't answer.

One Decade Ago

I was on a plane when I finally sat down to read the article when my imagination heard the words in her voice. *Exploitation. Abuse both mental and physical. Illegal videoing and public release of non-consensual porn for profit. Blackmail. Extortion. Solicitation and promotion of prostitution.*

And our names, mine, Ryder's, Finn's, and Jameson's, were all over the article. She'd named us each specifically, but factually, she was way off base. I hadn't pandered or solicited, promoted, released, abused, taped, extorted, or exploited anything. Like the women in the videos, I was a victim. Not that Avery would ever see it. How could she when she wouldn't even talk to me to hear my side of the story?

I reclined my seat and shut down the article on the tablet I was supposed to be using to learn plays. As soon as we landed, I was going to call her, convince her of my innocence, that had I known what they were doing, I would've stopped it. As much as I hoped she would listen, there was no way she was going to answer her phone and I couldn't blame her. Not after the party. After the way, they'd laughed at her and the comments that had been made.

I wanted to hold her, to whisk her away from all of it, to tell her I loved her and needed her and that I would do whatever it took to make this better for us.

And when the flight landed, I made the first of a thousand calls to her. Left the first of a thousand voicemails. Begged her to listen the first of a thousand times.

It was when I was in the locker room after a long and grueling practice that Sheriff Max Greenwell of the Levy County Florida Sheriff's Department served me with restraining and cease and desist orders signed by a Maine judge and expedited to me. Under penalty of law, I was forbidden from contacting Avery Stroh in any form; physically, by telephone, mail, or electronically.

So, I did the only thing I could do. I let her go.

Chapter 25

Avery

After a few hours of moping, a couple bouts of tears, and a dozen aborted text messages, I sat on my sofa with no idea how to fix the mess I'd made. But the doorbell chimed, and I stood, hopeful that Keaton had come back.

Instead, I opened the door to find Alex.

"I brought beer." He held up a six-pack and walked in past me.

And Susie. "I brought pizza."

She carried the box through the door.

And Jameson. "I didn't bring anything."

He slid around me to stand with the others.

And Keaton. "I brought them."

He leaned against the frame and waited for me to invite him in. I didn't have any idea what the hell was going on, but I turned to find them all seated around my table. Alex smiled at me. "You messed up everything."

Apparently, he'd come to insult me, to point out my flaws and add insult to the loads of injuries present in this day. But he was smiling, as was Susie.

"We need to talk." She stood and motioned for me to take her chair at my table, and I gave it a good long look before I sat. "Good."

Alex nodded. "I lied to you."

Didn't that figure? "I am not having an affair with Susie."

Well, that was good news. "Okay, but why would you say you are?"

Susie looked at Jameson. "It was my fault."

Jameson put a hand on her arm. "No. It was my fault."

"Oh, for the love of God." Alex shook his head, exasperated. "Susie and I have been friends forever. When you stopped spray painting the Alpha house with her, I picked up the ceremonial paint can and went penis wild, so to speak."

I stared, from one to the other, I wondered why he hadn't ever told me. Then it occurred to me. After I stopped spray-painting bad words on the front of their house, I started seeing Keaton and stopped seeing my friends. I added that to the list of my innumerable faults I couldn't fix in this situation and I was tired of it all.

So tired I would've ended the whole thing in favor of a nap, but Keaton was standing so close…smelled so good…made me want to hear the rest.

"Okay. You painted. And you and Susie got closer. What does that have to do with anything?" But if we could speed the whole thing up...

"Well, it didn't then, all that matters is that we've been friends since then. So I called him because I was having a rough time in my marriage. Jameson and I needed...something. We were losing the fight to want to be together. Not just the fight. We were even losing the will to put up the fight." Susie laid her hand on Jameson's cheek. "I'm a fighter, Avery, and Jameson is a fighter. But we needed to get our fight back."

"So, as a friend, I offered to help." Alex twisted his mouth to the side.

"I got punched in the face for it, too." He rubbed his jaw.

"Jealousy is a powerful motivator." Jameson nodded at me as if we shared this truth. He nodded at Keaton, too, then went back to smiling at Susie. "And I was jealous."

They took turns filling in details so that my head might as well have been on a swivel.

"And for a minute, I was confused." Susie laced her fingers with Jameson's and gave a squeeze. "But just a minute."

"And the ring I showed you was Grandma's." He looked down at his hands. "And I do love you, forever, but when I said I loved you, that night at the pier, it was me trying to throw you off Susie's trail. I didn't want you going to Jameson."

"And when you called me on it all…I knew we had to come clean." Susie smiled softly at Jameson then at me. "Especially when Keaton said…"

My eyes narrowed and her story stuttered. "What he said."

I looked up at Keaton. He hadn't moved closer, nor had he moved away. Right now, he was just there. A few feet that might as well have been a few miles. But more important than where he was, what had he said?

The weird lies between Jameson and Susie and Alex didn't affect me and Keaton or the things we had said to each other. We'd made such a mess of things between us, unresolved feelings, anger, harsh words and truths. No matter how well things worked for Susie and Jameson, and even Alex, there were no guarantees for me and Keaton and the thought broke my heart all over again.

One Decade Ago

In the space of one night, devastating as it was, everything changed. Or maybe it went back to normal, back to solitary me. It was back to my black-on-black wardrobe and back to the long stares and whispers when I passed.

Dean Ferguson tracked me down in the library. She looked haggard, run-down, and flustered, just like I felt. In fairness, this had been hard on her. The administration, the alumni, the students, all made their very public protests when the announcement was made about the suspensions and expulsions of half the football team. This was a talented team that brought home championships, trophies, bowl wins and you know, boys would be boys. The athletic association called for her resignation.

Damn the girls who'd been hurt and come forward. And the one, me, who'd pressed charges probably should've kept her clothes on or her mouth shut because she certainly didn't seem to mind what was going on in the video…and there was no evidence of force…and how could she not know she was on camera? I'd heard it all in the last few days.

"Miss Stroh?"

I looked up, swallowing a batch of tears because since this all started, I was always fighting tears.

"Is there somewhere we can talk?"

I had no home, just enough money to manage a meal a day when I wasn't working, and the nightly rate at the Come and Go motel.

I looked up from my paper on life choices

and consequences in *Pretty Woman*. "Not really."

She pulled out the chair across from me and folded her hands in front of her. "The Board of Regents is being pressured by the Association for Personal Integrity," one of those student-run clubs that judged and would've publicly flogged those they deemed unsavory if it had been lawful "to dismiss you for your part…in the umm…"

She looked at her hands then at me. "Video."

I nodded because I didn't know what to say. Without this school and my scholarship, I would end up back in Farmville, Illinois, working my shift as a sandwich artist at the local sub shop.

"My part in the video," I repeated her words but with the bite of disdain for the very notion that I'd been a willing accomplice in their stupidity. "I went to the police and filed a report, but with the boat burned and the Alpha house cleaned out already, the chances that they can prove who made the video or that it was uploaded without my permission are slim." That was what they'd told me anyway. Although I suspected that these avid football fans weren't really all that interested in helping me and all Alex and his computer guru buddies had been able to prove was that the IP address for the upload was on campus.

"Either way, if I can't prove I didn't have a part in the video creation process, they won't be able to suggest I did." Well, they could suggest whatever they wanted. "Not and make it stick, anyway."

She nodded and sighed. "The Alpha athletes have issued a formal apology for the behavior of their brothers." Yeah. I'd received a written copy of said apology, it lacked any form of sincerity, but it was better than nothing. "I don't have any choice but to reopen their house."

Of course, she didn't. "I know."

She laid her hand over mine. "I just want to say, you've been very brave through all of this, is there anything I can do for you?"

I smiled. "I could use dorm housing."

Her brow wrinkled and she slid her tongue along the line of her lower lip. "The dorms are full, presently, but I live in faculty housing and I have a spare room. If that would help." She shrugged. "I just don't want to see you give up now, you're so close."

My own family had done nothing for me, probably didn't even know where I'd ended up after high school. But here was this woman, this stranger, fighting for me, offering me a place to stay, and my eyes filled with tears. Maybe I just needed to get the emotions I'd been holding in out. Or maybe I was just tired, but I cried. Then I went to the motel, packed my three new shirts and two pairs of jeans into a bag, and moved them into her faculty college.

Chapter 26

Keaton

I watched Avery as she listened to this half-brained tale. She stared at Alex and Susie, not buying this ridiculous, but apparently truthful, story. I didn't care what she believed, I didn't care about anything but figuring out if we move beyond our past to create a future. I also needed them to leave so Avery and I could talk about it. But before I could suggest that they all leave, there was another knock at the door. Avery looked at each of us before she stood.

"Everyone I know is in this room." and her chuckle was more wry than joyous as she shook her head and walked to the door.

Ryder didn't wait to be asked in and shoved past her. "Oh good. The gang's all here." Jameson looked at me, his eyes wide and wary, while Avery crossed her arms and shot Ryder a glare that should have melted his skin from his bones. He walked toward the table and I stopped his forward progress with my body. "Hey, tough guy. Just wanna talk to your girl."

He reeked of alcohol and leaned a little too far left as he cocked his head so that he looked like he was trying to lean against a wall where there was none.

Avery stepped around me. "What do you want, Ryder?"

He looked her up and down, frowned, and glanced at me.

"I don't know." His mouth twitched. "I just don't know."

Even as he seemed to deflate, I didn't trust

him and moved to stand beside her. I hadn't been able to protect her from his behavior ten years ago, but now, I would do whatever it took to keep anyone from hurting her. He sat heavily on the couch and puffed his cheeks to blow out a breath.

"Did you know, the only time I was happy was in college?" Avery watched him but didn't speak. "And then I met you."

He shoved his finger toward her. "Do you remember that? I was mowing grass at the Chaplain's house."

Avery nodded. "Yeah. I'd just got to campus."

"I carried a box for you." He sniffed and leaned forward to rest his elbows on his knees. "I was going to ask you out, but you lived above their garage."

"I had such a crush on you, I asked Keaton to help me, I wanted to turn into someone you would want."

He chuckled. "You were the one girl I

couldn't figure out, and then all of a sudden, you're spending all this time with him, smiling *at him*, kissing *him*, spending the night on his dad's boat with *him.*" He shot a glance at me. "I was so jealous."

Avery crossed her arms.

"That's why I goaded him into the bet, and I made sure you knew about it. I wanted to hurt him, to make him hurt you. I thought I would be able to rush in and pick up the pieces after you found out about the bet and the video. I thought you would blame him."

All this was because he was jealous? Because he was too chickenshit to ask her out himself? I glanced at Avery who was buying every second of this bullshit.

"Why didn't you just tell me?" She asked, doubt in every inch of her face.

"You wanted him." He jerked his finger toward me.

"So, you decided to humiliate me? To have me almost kicked out of school?" She screeched, and despite how much it hurt my ears, I couldn't blame her.

He blew out a breath and nodded, blood roared in my ears. He'd ruined everything.

"And he got you anyway." Ryder wasn't even listening to her anymore. Or looking at her. "He got everything I ever wanted."

Avery's mouth dropped open. "Are you kidding me, right now?" She shook her head. "You almost ruined my life, you definitely ruined my relationship with Keaton." She turned to me.

"I was hurt when I wrote the article. All I could see was all those people laughing at me, watching me on those TVs in the Alpha house, thinking you were a hero and I was this pathetic chick who…" She shook her head and cleared her throat. "I don't know what I thought. All I knew was I was hurt and I thought…"

"You could've talked to me. I would've… explained." I wanted to touch her but kept my hands curled in my pockets. "I would've told you I didn't know about the videos or that he was going to play it."

She nodded and her voice softened as she laid her hand on my chest. "I know."

Ryder stood. "Oh look. He's gonna get the girl again."

I shot him a glare. I didn't give a fuck about Ryder or what he said, I didn't care about his jealousy or the fact if he wanted her back then, he could've tried to date her. And he probably would've succeeded, all I cared about was that she was standing so close to me and I gave up the right to touch her, to be with her when I challenged her motives when I forced her to choose between me and her friendship with Alex.

She glanced at Ryder then at me then back to him. "There was a time when I would've sold my soul to hear you say you wanted me. When I would've turned myself inside out to be with you."

And now, I wasn't sure whether she was talking to me or to him.

"But you hurt me and there's no excuse for what you did, no way can I forgive you." And this time I was almost sure she was talking to me. "I was never going to be enough for you."

"That isn't true," I whispered the words. "You were always more than I deserved. More than I knew what to do with."

She gazed at me, smiling, shaking her head, holding out her hand. "I should've talked to you before I wrote that article."

"I should've never given you a reason to write it."

Ryder blew a pfft between his teeth. "What about me? I lost everything, my education, my chance at a pro career, my best friend, and the girl of my dreams."

I ignored him and pulled Avery close, I needed her and I would spend every day making the last ten years up to her, savoring every minute we had together.

Epilogue

Avery

"Do you, Avery Leticia Stroh, take Keaton to be your lawfully wedded husband?" He scrunched up his nose as he mimicked the judge who'd married us. The man's voice had been tinny and thin, nothing like that of the dreamboat of a groom trying to sound like him now. "I was so scared she was going to say no." He chuckled. "Almost peed my pants."

He glanced at Susie and Jameson, then at Alex, and finally at Finn who had pitched the idea of our story to a movie producer out west, and now we were knee-deep in writing the script. Together with Keaton and Jameson as helpers.

Keaton lifted his glass and covered my hand with his free one. "I love you, Avery. Now and forever."

We all drank, and Keaton leaned in to kiss me.

Jameson waited until we parted then smiled. "Ryder's standing at the bar."

Of course, he was. But I had something to say, I winked at Keaton and nodded to his former best friend. "I'll be right back."

Before I made it a step, he slid an arm around my waist. "Am I going to need bail money?"

I chuckled and kissed his cheek. "We'll see." But I doubted it. When I slid into the spot beside Ryder, I ordered a beer. "And get one for him, too."

Ryder looked down at me and sighed. "Thanks."

"What you did to me sucked."

He nodded. "I know." He took a long drink of his beer, finishing it then picked up the one I'd just bought. "Trust me. I'm well aware and I wish…"

"Back then, I thought it was the worst thing that could ever happen to me. But, after graduation, I saw you sweeping the street for the city. Not a bad job, but not what you hoped for."

He half-smiled.

"No. Nothing turned out the way I hoped." He shrugged. "For what it's worth, I'm sorry for what I did to you, so sorry."

After all these years, that was really all I wanted to hear. I'd gotten over the embarrassment because the bruhaha over the video lasted about one minute in the grand scheme of my life. The scandal faded, people moved on, graduated, found jobs that took them away. I also figured out how to be okay with who I was, how not to want to change myself every time someone didn't like something about me. I found that happiness in spite of, or maybe because of the video, it showed me I was strong enough to survive.

"I know, you should come over and have a drink." He cocked an eyebrow. "What you did is only part of who you are. You were all friends once and if he cared about you, that must mean there's something redeemable about you. I trust his judgment."

He'd been punished, served his sentence, lost the life he'd dreamed of, and to move on completely, I could forgive him.

And I could watch him laugh with my husband, joke with his friends, and not be hurt. Our lives moved on and I was happy…happier when Keaton pulled me close and held me, kissed me, and promised me forever. Again. And this time, I was holding him to it.

About Summer Cooper

Thank you so much for reading. Without you, it wouldn't be possible for me to be a full-time author. I hope you enjoy reading my books as much as I do writing them.

Besides (obviously!) reading and writing, I also love cuddling my dogs, shouting at Alexa, being upside down (aka Yoga) and driving my family cray-cray!

Get in touch at
hello@summercooper.com
www.summercooper.com

Made in the USA
Middletown, DE
23 November 2024

65274388R00184